SAINT'S GROVE SERIES

Immortal Ties by Jennifer Malone Wright

Heart's Aligning by Miranda Hardy

Her Forbidden Knight by Carly Fall

Racing Time by Elizabeth Kirke

Crossing Time by M.H. Soars

Across the Universe by Elise Marion

The Ghost and the Belle by Rose Shababy

All Dragons' Eve by Casse NaRome

Worlds Apart by Amy Richie

Heart by Sharon Stevenson

Enchanted Souls by Tia Silverthorne Bach

Thy Heart's Desire by P.T. Macias

THE GHOST AND THE BELLE

ROSE SHABABY

First Edition: June 2016
Library of Congress Cataloging-in-Publication Data

Rose Shababy
The Ghost and the Belle
A SAINT'S GROVE SERIES NOVEL
ISBN-13: 978-0-9904620-4-0

*"This book is for everyone who believes
that love and magic are sometimes the very same thing."*

PROLOGUE

Saint's Grove, VA, September 9th, 1875

Benjamin Churchill bent over his large but plain wooden desk, his untidy chestnut locks falling across his face despite the thin leather thong he used to tie it back. One piece of hair drifted across his cheek and he reached up to push it away, his fingers ruffling the several days of beard growth on his chin.

You better shave that before Stella sees it, he told himself.

Of course, he usually had at least a shadow of a beard covering his strong square jaw. He often forgot to shave, and his perpetually messy hair constantly fell in his eyes. His attire suffered a similar fate, often wrinkled and shirts half tucked in. On any other man it would have been a messy and unappealing sight, but Benjamin managed to give off an alluring, albeit casual, rakish charm that had most of the young women in town tittering behind their gloved hands when he walked by. Perhaps it was the glint in his eye, his strong, even white teeth that sparkled when he smiled, or the way his shirt never managed to hide his muscular strength. To all those young women he'd been viewed as the most eligible bachelor in town.

Tucking a loose piece of hair behind an ear, his chocolate brown eyes squinted as the light of the kerosene lamp glowed gently on the papers in front of him.

More papers littered his desk, and several nibs lay strewn about, as well as a nearly empty inkwell. He pored over the papers, pursing his perfectly-shaped, almost too-full-for-a-man lips.

A recent graduate from the University of Virginia School of Law, summa cum laude no less, the loan papers he now studied represented the most important case of his short career as a lawyer. He'd enjoyed his time at university, but Benjamin was a man who knew his mind. From the beginning he planned on coming back to his home town of Saint's Grove to set up shop, and nothing swayed him from his course. Not even the beauty and intellectual pursuits found in Charlottesville were enough to replace the picturesque charm of Saint's Grove, or his love of the small town.

His parents both passed away before he finished college, and he nearly had to beg, borrow and steal to hold onto the family home for both him and his brother Armin. A plain man, he was a year younger than Benjamin. Armin possessed a kind but simple nature and always managed better when he had someone telling him what to do. The brothers lived together in their childhood home, Benjamin providing the income and Armin taking care of most of the daily chores.

Benjamin converted the downstairs of the house into his office when he set up his practice. It consisted of two large rooms: the foyer, which stretched into the back of the house and now served as his personal office space, and what used to be the dining room, which sat to the side of the foyer and now held his library. Plain green brocade curtains hung in all the windows, including the large bay window facing the town square. All the curtains were drawn, and other than the kerosene lamp, the only other light in the room came from the fire crackling in the fireplace along the wall opposite the library.

He arrived home, anxious to share his newfound skills with the townsfolk and benefit the community as a whole. Unfortunately, in the year since he established his law office, his most exciting job had been when he prepared the last will and testament for old lady Harrelson.

Until Jedediah Hawkins burst into his office almost in tears.

Rail thin and weathered, Jed owned one of the farms on the outskirts of town. It was a beautiful homestead where he raised cattle, grew apples and tobacco, and lived with his wife and three children.

The two men were only a couple years apart and had attended primary school together. Although Benjamin never thought of Jed as a close friend, he had always liked him and knew him to be an honest, considerate man.

Jed possessed a very small savings when he found the farm of his dreams nestled along the base of the Blue Ridge Mountains. Unwilling to let it slip through his fingers, he went to Stone's Banking and Loan, Saint's Grove one and only bank, and secured a loan. He'd paid his mortgage faithfully for ten years, until the previous month when he went in to make his usual payment, only to be told they were calling in his loan.

Jed begged them to reconsider, but to no avail, finally bringing him to Benjamin's doorstep.

"I don't understand," he almost sobbed as he sat across from Benjamin. "How can they just take a man's life away without so much as a how-di-do? I've never missed a payment." Jed buried his face in his hands, muffling his words. "What am I going to tell Carol Anne and the kids?"

Benjamin knew exactly what happened the moment he looked at the loan papers. "Jed," he swallowed, barely able to look at the other man. "There's a term call option in your loan agreement."

Jed stared at him blankly.

Benjamin sighed, running a hand through his hair. "The bank stipulated that they can review your loan every five years and demand payment in full rather than continue the loan. It's in writing and you signed it. The second five years comes up next month."

Jed paled, moaning a little. "I didn't know. How the heck would I? Surely there is something you can do. Perhaps you could talk to the bank?"

Benjamin shrugged a little. "I'll attempt it, but my honest opinion is that it will be fruitless." He held up a hand when Jed began to weep in earnest. "Do not worry, Jed. I'll do what I can to help you."

And he did. He went to the bank, talked to the loan officer who barely met his gaze as he dismissed Benjamin with a casual disregard.

Benjamin didn't stop there. He made an appointment

with the owner of the bank, Marlon Stone.

Stone was a large man, his scarlet silk cravat tucked into shirt, his rich velvet vest stretched tight across his belly. His jowls quivered slightly as he eyed Benjamin across the immense walnut desk that dominated his office.

"How may I help you, young man?" he asked with a hint of condescension.

Benjamin felt a muscle in his jaw tick. "I wanted to speak with you about Jed Hawkins."

"Ah, yes," Stone brightened. "Are you here to pay his loan?"

"No, I'm here to ask you to reconsider calling it in."

"Reconsider?" Stone's bushy eyebrows furrowed. "Why on earth would I do that?"

Benjamin fought the urge to curse, the only hint of his frustration in his flared nostrils. "Jedediah is an asset to the community. He employs several farmhands, all local boys, sells his crops locally as well as throughout the state, and as he continues to grow and his crops reach their full potential, he'll put Saint's Grove on the map as one of the largest tobacco farmers in the state. Retaining our local businessmen is vital to this town." He smiled at the older man. "Besides, surely you are not in need of the money, and what would a man like you do with a farm?"

"True, I'm in no need of the money personally." Stone nodded, reaching for a wooden box on his desk and withdrawing a large cigar. He clipped the end, lighting it. He puffed for a moment before pointing at Benjamin. "Nevertheless, we here at Stone's Banking and Loan have been offering far too many loans. We're stretched too thin these days and it would only take one big financial crisis to pull us under. No, I'm sorry. There's simply nothing I can do."

"Nothing you *can* do, or nothing you *will* do?" Benjamin gritted out, regretting the words as soon as they came out of his mouth.

Stone's eyes turned to flint. "In this case, they are synonymous."

Benjamin studied the man, his rich clothing, gold rings and diamond pin in his cravat, and fought the anger welling inside him. "Are you calling in all your loans?"

"Well, now, that's bank business," Stone harrumphed. "I'm not at liberty to discuss such things. No, I'm sorry, young man. I'm afraid you've wasted your time. There's simply nothing I can do," he repeated.

He stood, indicating the meeting was over.

Benjamin stayed seated for a moment. "Mr. Stone, can you really justify putting a family out of their home? Jed's children were born and raised there. What possible use would you have for their farm?"

Stone's face hardened, and eyes darkened further, something in them almost frightening Benjamin. He'd never liked the banker, but now he felt something ominous coming off the older man.

And he was certain there was much more going on with the farm than either he or Jed knew. He didn't know how he knew, but every instinct inside him was screaming at him, telling him that Stone had an ulterior motive.

Benjamin stood to leave, determined to find out what Stone really wanted with the farm. "Thank you for your time," he told the banker. "I'll be seeing you."

Now, sitting at his desk, he pushed the loan papers aside in frustration.

"Damn him!" Benjamin slammed a fist down on his

desk, the inkwell jumping from the force. He buried his face in his hands. He desperately wanted to help Jed, but for all his desire, he knew there was nothing he could do. Never in his life had he felt like such an utter failure.

The door to his office swung open, a cold wind sweeping through the room, causing the flame in the lamp on his desk to flicker wildly and papers to flutter. He clamped a strong hand down on them as he looked up at the young woman entering.

"Sorry!" she trilled, closing the door quickly. She was a tall and slender woman with features like delicate china and pale blonde hair piled high on her head underneath a stylishly high blue hat decorated with frills and ribbons that matched her dress. She smiled at Benjamin, accentuating her high cheekbones and nearly taking his breath away with her beauty.

He smiled back at her and stood to greet her as she crossed the room and lightly kissed his cheek. "Stella, darling, I wasn't expecting you."

Stella reached up behind her tall bonnet to remove her hatpin, placing both the pin and the hat on his desk. "I wanted to visit my fiancée." She beamed at him and Benjamin felt a surge of emotion. He wrapped his arms around her, pulling her against his hard chest and letting his lips trail across hers. She responded in kind, letting her hands wander to his hair.

Passion stirred low in Benjamin's gut a moment later and he gently pushed her away. "Temptress," he muttered hoarsely. "I believe you do this to me on purpose. Our marriage cannot come soon enough."

Her eyes twinkled as she widened them in feigned innocence. "I don't know what you mean."

"You're a terrible liar."

Her gaze drifted down to his chin and a tiny frown turned the corners of her mouth down. "I see you've been so busy you've forgotten to take care of yourself again. Don't let father see you like that. You know how much importance he puts on appearance."

Stella's father owned Pennington Dry Goods in the town square. A fastidious man, Mr. Pennington always seemed to vaguely disapprove of Benjamin. He believed strongly that a man should be composed and well put together, and a disheveled appearance such as Benjamin's was a direct contradiction of that belief. Of course, Stella constantly tried to get him to dress better, to pay more attention to his appearance. It was one of the qualities he liked least about her.

Still, Benjamin found himself entranced by her beauty and her father hadn't been able to stop the growing romance between them after Benjamin returned from school.

Even though they'd grown up in the same town, Stella was several years younger than him and still in pigtails when he left for school. He'd never given much thought to the scrawny girl who worked with her father at the dry goods prior to leaving for the university, but when he returned he was shocked to find that she had grown into a winsome beauty.

Before long the two had pledged their love to one another and Benjamin had asked her father's permission to propose, something Mr. Pennington had granted grudgingly. He didn't entirely approve of Benjamin, but he loved his daughter and wanted her to be happy.

Benjamin pulled the leather thong out of his hair and attempted to pull it all back and retie it. "I have most defi-

THE GHOST AND THE BELLE

nitely been neglecting my appearance and I know you think I'm a wretch. I'll shave tonight."

"See that you do." Her cheeks dimpled as she smiled. "Where's Armin?"

He shrugged. "He told me he was going to the dry goods for a few supplies, so I'm surprised you didn't see him before you came. If he wasn't at the store, I can't say where he's gotten to." He smiled. "You know Armin."

She nodded. "And how are things coming along with your case? Have you saved poor Mr. Hawkins' farm?"

Benjamin frowned. "Sadly, no. I have one more lead to follow up, but if it doesn't prove fruitful, I'm afraid there isn't much I can do for him. I'm not hopeful."

She placed a sympathetic hand on his shoulder. "How unfortunate. There's nothing, then?"

He let his gaze turn to the papers strewn across his desk, tapping a fist on the wood. "Not that I can tell." He shook his head in frustration. "I spoke with Mr. Stone and he simply wasn't willing to budge, although something about his demeanor made me uncomfortable so I went down to the town hall and looked up current ownership of the property surrounding Jed's. Mr. Stone has recently acquired a new partner, a company called SP Enterprises. Together, they've purchased several large plots of land around the Hawkins' farm over the course of the last year, none of which were mortgaged by the bank. I looked at the property values of those pieces of land and found he paid far above market value for them. Now he's after Jed's land. It's all very suspicious. I believe he wants that land for a specific reason."

"SP Enterprises? I don't know them." Stella's fine brow wrinkled.

"Neither do I, but I'll be going down to the court-house tomorrow to investigate. I'd like to know who's behind the company."

"And what possible reason would they have for a bunch of old farms?"

"I do not know. I have my suspicions, but they're vague at best."

"What do you suspect?"

He shrugged. "Perhaps something on the land itself is of interest to him. It is the only explanation I can come up with. As such, I've sent off for geological surveys of the land. I expect them any day now."

"Geological survey?" Stella raised an eyebrow. "What use will that be?"

"Perhaps none. And if it proves fruitless, that will be the end of things for Jed." His face darkened. "If I have to tell the man there's no hope of saving his farm, I would at least like to be able to tell him I did all I could to help him."

Stella glanced down at her dress, smoothing an imaginary wrinkle. "You certainly can't be faulted for your thoroughness."

He turned away, placing his clenched fists on the edge of the front of the desk. His head sagged a bit as a huge sigh ran through him with a shudder. "I feel like I've failed him."

"Oh, I'm sure you'll find something," Stella muttered, a dark look crossing her face.

Benjamin frowned. Something about her tone made him uneasy. Normally a winsome girl, her reaction seemed unusual. "I'm not sure I understand your meaning."

She glanced at him and brightened slightly. "I meant

nothing, my dear. I'm certain no matter the outcome, Mr. Hawkins will underst—"

The front door of the office swung open, and three men with handkerchiefs pulled up over their faces burst into the room, cutting Stella off midsentence. A cold wind rushed through the room just as before, except this time the papers on Benjamin's desk swirled madly around the room as the lamp on the desk flickered and went out. One of the men slammed the door shut behind them as the other two trained pistols on both Benjamin and Stella.

The only light left in the room came from the fireplace, the flames crackling as their light played across the furniture, casting ominous shadows all around the room.

Benjamin instinctively stepped in front of Stella. "Who are you?" he asked, his voice clipped and angry.

The man who had closed the door marched across the room and backhanded Benjamin so hard he staggered backward, knocking Stella to the ground. She cried out and Benjamin immediately knelt down to help her up.

"Shut up!" the man snarled.

"I'm sorry, darling," Benjamin tried to sooth Stella as she looked up at him with frightened eyes. "Are you all right? Did I hurt you?"

She shook her head. "N-n-no, I'm fine," she managed.

He turned to stare up at the men. "What do you want?" he snarled.

The two men brandishing guns moved across the room quickly, tearing him away from Stella while the third man, clearly the ringleader, grabbed her arm and roughly hauled her up off the floor. She began crying in earnest and something wild erupted in Benjamin.

"Get your filthy hands off her!" he roared, struggling to get away from his captors. He pulled with all his might, escaping their grasp and rushing forward to attack the man holding Stella. As he neared them, the man pulled a strange looking knife from his belt and plunged it into his chest.

"Benjamin!" Stella screamed.

He looked down to see the knife jutting out of his chest, the hilt an ornate, strangely shaped piece of silver. He reached up and grasped the handle, screaming hoarsely as he pulled it out of his chest. A crimson stain spreading across the linen of his shirt as all his strength seemed to leave his body, and he fell to his knees, one hand reaching for the sobbing woman in front of him. "Stella," he gasped. His vision narrowed, as if he looked down a dark tunnel, and the last thing he saw was the masked man holding his fiancée, lifting a gun to her head as her eyes wide with terror and tears streamed down her face.

CHAPTER ONE

"*My dear fellow,*" *said Sherlock Holmes as we sat on either side of the fire in his lodgings at Baker Street, "life is infinitely stranger than anything which the mind of man could invent. We would not dare to conceive the things which are really mere commonplaces of existence. If we could fly out of that window hand in hand, hover over this great city, gently remove the roofs, and peep in at the queer things which are going on, the strange coincidences, the plannings, the cross-purposes, the wonderful chains of events, working through generation, and leading to the most outre results, it would make all fiction with its conventionalities and foreseen conclusions most stale and unprofitable.*"

The jingle jangle of the brass bells attached to the front door of the store jarred Irene Bell from the pages of her book. She sighed, glanced longingly at the worn hardback one more time before marking her place with a magnifying glass shaped bookmark. "Later, Mr. Holmes," she whispered.

She pushed her coal black mess of curls away from her face as she rose from her stool behind the cash register. "Good morning," she welcomed the young man walking toward her. He had a pleasant face and wore khakis with a polo shirt. *Another college kid,* she guessed as she continued her greeting. "Welcome to Sherlock's Tomes. May I help you find something?"

He glanced around, his eyes taking in the natural wood paneling and the overflowing bookshelves as he walked toward her. The old floorboards creaked as he came toward her and she leaned across the counter, smiling in what she hoped was a friendly, courteous way.

"Yes," he nodded. He smiled easily, clearly portraying his interest as he studied her fine-boned features. "I'm working on a paper for my cultural anthropology class at SGCC."

Nailed it! Irene bit down on her tongue to hold back a laugh. "Professor McGurty's class?"

The young man nodded again. "It's a comparative study on the religious and ethical practices of another culture, and how they relate to contemporary American values." A grin swept across his face, and he flashed pearly white teeth at her. "I thought perhaps one of the indigenous tribes of South America or Africa."

Irene bit her full bottom lip a little, suppressing a laugh. It happened every year, with each new group of students. Professor McGurty's cultural anthropology class at Saint's Grove Community College, and each year he gave them the same comparative study as their first research paper. The students never realized that the real study was their own interpretation of contemporary American values. Professor McGurty handed out anonymous versions of the assignment, asking the students to create a profile about the author's value system based on the assumptions made in their research paper, sometimes with very interesting results.

Of course, as the proprietor of the only bookstore in town, Irene had been privy to the assignment for years. Professor McGurty had sworn her to secrecy from the beginning.

"I think I have exactly what you're looking for," Irene told the young man. She came around the counter. Holding out a hand, she directed him to toward the back of the store, leading him to a room in the far left back corner of the building. "Most of my research books are in here. I work with the college to keep specific titles on hand." She led him to a shelf and removed several volumes. "One of these should work."

He took the books, studying them for a few moments before choosing one. "This appears used. Do you offer buy backs?"

"No, but you can return it for store credit," she explained.

"Fair enough," His gaze swept down the length of her body and Irene flushed. "May I help you with anything else today?" she asked politely, suppressing a frown as well as the urge to cross her arms over her chest. It was the same old story. How many times had a man looked at her the same way? Despite the jeans and loose sweater she wore, she knew there was no disguising her generous curves. She had grown used to it, but that didn't mean she liked it.

"No, I think this is all I need for now." He followed

her back to the register. She flushed as she walked, and knew he was studying her backside.

She rang up the book, putting it in a paper bag. "That will be thirty-one fifty-eight."

"I'm Ethan, by the way," he told her as he handed her two twenties.

She took the money. "Irene."

"Are you excited about the eclipse tonight?" he asked her as she counted back his change.

For months, every news station in the country had been buzzing with reports of the upcoming stellar phenomenon. Not only was a full lunar eclipse predicted, but scientists also claimed that six of the planets in the solar system would fall into alignment at exactly the same moment.

The citizens of Saint's Grove had been planning for the spectacle for months, organizing a picnic in the town square so they could watch the event.

Irene shrugged. "I haven't really thought about it much," she answered.

"Are you going to the picnic?" He leaned against the counter again, hope written across his face.

"I hadn't planned on it."

"Perhaps you've been waiting for the right companion?" His eyes gleamed with invitation.

"Perhaps not," she answered coolly. "But thank you anyway."

He straightened, disappointment gracing his features. "Well, here's my number, if you change your mind." He wrote it on a slip of paper and handed it to her.

"Will do." She waited until the front door closed behind him, then threw the slip of paper in the metal trash bin under the counter. *Why*? She wondered. *Why can't I just once meet a man who's more interested in my mind than my body?*

Glancing at the clock, she noted with relief that it was nearly closing time and started her nightly routine. Irene grabbed a broom and dustpan tucked away behind the counter and began sweeping the floor, making her way from room to room with brisk efficiency.

When she reached the bathroom in the right corner of the building, she retrieved a container of cleaning wipes and gave the entire bathroom a quick scrub down.

She stopped to study herself in the mirror for a moment, trying to see the same thing men saw when they looked at her. Objectively, she knew she possessed full pink lips, pearly teeth, a petite nose with just the slightest upward slant, high cheekbones, doe-like green eyes, and a curvy hourglass figure. She also knew she looked more like one of the models on the cover of a romance novel than the bibliophile she was.

"Why?" she muttered to herself, squeezing her eyes shut. *Why couldn't I just look like a regular woman? Why this freakish caricature?*

Always shy and bookish, Irene had been mortified when she began developing at thirteen. By the time she reached sixteen, she looked twenty and had to adjust to grown men leering and hitting on her in public. She had no idea how to deal with it, however, and so she retreated into her books. She refused all advances from everyone, even boys her own age, certain they all wanted her only for the way she looked. As a result, she'd never even been on a date in her entire life, let alone had a boyfriend.

A situation that left her untouched as a woman of

twenty-six.

Her mother hadn't been much help either. Just as shy and bookish as Irene, Kathleen Bell had a slim figure and little idea how to help her daughter. A quietly, albeit cliché, unassuming librarian, her only experience with men had been the one brief love affair with Irene's father, resulting in a whirlwind marriage and eventually, Irene.

Joseph Bell abandoned them when Irene was just a baby, and Kathleen never spoke of him. Instead, she raised her daughter in a quiet household and it never really occurred to Irene to ask about her paternal family.

A mistake, she realized later, when her mother died in a tragic car accident a couple months after her sixteenth birthday. The state of Virginia looked for her father, only to discover he had gone missing years before and her only remaining relative was his much older sister, Caroline.

Aunt Caroline agreed to take her, and the next thing Irene knew, she was moving across state, far from her hometown of Norfolk, to the tiny mountain town of Saint's Grove.

Caroline had no children but she'd taught English at the community college until her retirement a few years earlier, so she seemed to understand Irene in a way her mother never had. After the first few awkward weeks they got along as well as if they'd known each other forever. Irene missed her mother, but she was grateful for the opportunity to get to know her aunt.

Fate, however, seemed to feel that Irene belonged alone, and Caroline passed away quietly in her sleep just after Irene graduated high school, leaving her the quaint Victorian home they lived in, as well as her life savings.

Savings enough for Irene to do what she wished with

herself, and she knew exactly what she wanted.

She continued to live in the same house and attended school to study business, determined to combine the knowledge she gained with her love of literature and open a bookstore. Four years later she did just that, turning the house into the bookstore and converting the upstairs into an apartment.

Another four years later, the store managed to turn enough of a profit to stay open and let Irene hermit herself away.

And it was the best decision I ever made, she told herself as she gazed in the mirror a moment longer before turning to leave the bathroom.

She put her broom away and went back to the counter to retrieve a feather duster from the shelf below the register. After locking the front door, she moved through the store quickly, swiping quickly across most surfaces, pausing only once. She stared down at the contents of a fine cherry wood frame hanging on the wall opposite of the register and next to the contemporary fiction room. Carefully protected by special UV glass and hung in the middle of the room to limit its exposure to sunlight, the frame held Irene's most prized possession: an original Beeton's Christmas Annual from 1887, turned to display the story 'A Study In Scarlet,' the very first time Sir Arthur Conan Doyle's Sherlock Holmes ever appeared in print.

Irene adored Sherlock Holmes. It didn't hurt that her great-great-great-great-grandfather had been Joseph Bell, one of Doyle's professors and the inspiration for Holmes, but beyond that, Irene loved Holmes' analytical nature. She loved how he didn't let emotion get in his way, how he could look at any situation with a fair and unbiased eye.

He seemed the epitome of a man, unconcerned with trifles like relationships in his pursuit of knowledge.

She often wished she had the ability to cut off her emotions in the same way.

Irene carefully dusted the top of the frame, making sure it was centered and even, before moving on as she indulged in a little light fantasizing about Holmes suddenly appearing before her and asking for her assistance in his latest case.

"You must," he would insist. "It is not without some great dismay and, I must add, a rather brutal blow to my ego, but I must admit I'm flummoxed. You, my dear Irene, are the only person on earth I can think of who possesses an eclectic base of knowledge as wide and varied as my own, as well as a similarly sharp eye and keen intellect."

Irene felt her face grow warm from the very thought as she laughed lightly. "My dear Holmes," she murmured. "If you can't solve the case, I don't see how I could be of any help to you. No one else has your powers of deduction."

He would grasp her hands in his, his eyes sparkling with need. "Perhaps, but I would feel better if you agreed to at least look at the meager evidence I've gathered."

Irene sighed a little, sinking down into a chair in the contemporary fiction room. *I'd give anything to find a man like Sherlock,* she thought. Sure, Holmes didn't get into relationships, nor did he suffer romantic fools, but in all his stories there was still one woman who managed to capture his interest. None other than, as it turned out, her namesake, Irene Adler, a woman possessing the same sharp intellect and steadiness as Holmes' himself.

Irene couldn't help but hope that she would have impressed him just as much.

She flushed suddenly as she realized she was acting like a lovesick teenager. "Enough silliness," she told herself, and continued with her chores, finally putting her duster away and shutting off the lights before gathering her book from earlier and ascending the stairs to her little apartment above the store.

CHAPTER TWO

Day One

I rene moved about her apartment, turning on lights and filling a kettle with water for chamomile tea.

The apartment followed a similar **floor** plan as the bookstore. The living room sat above the foyer, the main bedroom off to the left and the kitchen, bathroom, and tiny spare room at the back.

The walls were painted in eggshell with a pale peach trim and most of the furniture in the apartment had belonged to her Aunt Caroline, hence it looked a little like an eighty-year-old woman lived there. Floral chintz and delicate doilies decorated the room. Irene didn't love the furniture, but she did love having the reminder of her aunt.

As the water for her tea heated, she prepared a tuna

sandwich and a small salad for her dinner. She thought about Ethan again, the young college boy from earlier who'd asked her out.

She hadn't been honest with him about her excitement over the upcoming eclipse. In truth, she'd been looking forward to it as much as anyone else. After all, a total lunar eclipse and the alignment of the planets was a sight to behold.

What she didn't look forward to was joining the entire town in the square to watch it. Instead, she planned on watching it from the privacy of her charming little balcony just off her bedroom. The balcony overlooked the town square, and there was enough room for two comfortable wicker lounge chairs and a small table, and included a scalloped overhang in case of rain.

Hardly a concern however, she realized as she plated her food, poured steaming water into her teacup, and opened the doors to the balcony.

The sun had begun to set behind the Blue Ridge Mountains off in the distance, filling the sky with brilliant oranges and pinks, highlighting the ethereal blue halo around the craggy peaks. Irene loved the mountains in the evening, and they were part of the reason she stayed after her Aunt Caroline passed away. Where else could she find a town with such quaint charm and natural beauty all around?

Placing her dinner on the little glass top patio table, Irene fetched the book she'd been reading and a lap blanket, then settled into one of the lounge chairs.

She nibbled on her sandwich and watched as the town square slowly filled with the residents of Saint's Grove. Street carts selling hot dogs, cotton candy, and snow cones

sat along the edge of the square while several street per-
formers wandered through the square.

The square was the pride and joy of the entire town.
Most of the town's municipal buildings and local businesses, almost all still in the original structures erected by
the town's founding fathers, surrounded the huge expanse
of lush green grass where the town put on concerts, weekly
farmer's markets, fairs and more. A statue of Peter Saint,
the founder of Saint's Grove, sat at the head of the square,
a reminder of their rich heritage.

The town had the distinction of being over three hundred years old. Originally a mining town, Saint's Grove
was steeped in urban legends and history involving ghosts,
demons, angels, vampires, werewolves, and witches.

Not that Irene gave and credence to such silly super-
stitions.

Families and couples arrived with blankets and lawn
chairs in tow. She watched as a number of people un-
packed picnic baskets or pulled containers of food from
bags and backpacks.

Small children ran through the grass, some barefoot
and dirty-faced as they hooted and hollered at each other.
She saw several children brandishing sticks like swords,
and a small group playing a vigorous game of tag.

Groups of teenagers slouched through the square
looking bored as they talked furtively to each other or bus-
ily tapped away at their cell phones.

Many of the businesses surrounding the square were
still open due to the special event, and the entire area began to fill with people looking in store windows, others
lingering outside the bar and coffeehouse, and even more
talking to friends and neighbors as they strolled along the

wide open walkways.

Irene recognized a number of people in the square. As the only bookstore in town, a huge number of residents came to her shop on a semi regular basis, but she was also familiar with most of the business owners and their employees of the shops that surrounded the town square.

Sipping her tea, she noticed a number of officers from the Saint's Grove police department wandering through the square in pairs. The SGPD usually made an appearance at town events, but as an outside observer, Irene could tell instantly there were more officers on duty than usual.

She wondered what Holmes would say about it. She could almost hear his rich tones.

"My dear Miss Bell," he muttered, thoughtfully plucking at his bottom lip. *"It is most abundantly clear that our local authorities expect much more than the forecasted celestial event."*

"What could they possibly be expecting?" she inquired. *"Saint's Grove is such a quiet little town with rarely more than a case of shoplifting."*

Holmes shook his head. *"That I cannot say at this juncture due to lack of evidence. However, if you like, we can find our way out into the square and observe the comings and goings of the townspeople. Perhaps then we will be able to deduce the expectations of your sheriff."*

"No," she said out loud. She had no desire to get out into the square and interact and was irritated with herself for the direction her little daydream had taken. *It's my daydream, for goodness sake,* she thought crossly.

Glancing up, she saw the moon climbing in the sky even though the sun hadn't fully set. A reddish hue had begun to creep up one side of it, casting an eerie pall everywhere she looked. Something about it made her feel strange and she shivered slightly.

Don't' be silly, she admonished herself and opened her book, turning to the short story she'd been reading earlier. She wondered what Sherlock Holmes would have to say about the eclipse, but refused to let herself daydream again.

At least for the moment.

Instead, she continued reading, munching on her salad and sandwich and sipping her tea until the food was gone and the teacup empty. Pulling her lap blanket around her legs, she sat back and let her mind become engrossed in the story.

It didn't take long before she felt her body relaxing, and her eyelids grow heavy. Placing the book on the table, she laid back and closed her eyes. *Just a little nap,* she promised herself. *Ten or fifteen minutes and then I'll clean up and get ready to watch the eclipse. I'm sure it's almost time.*

"Irene. Irene!"

She heard the urgency behind the voice calling her name and opened her eyes.

Standing above her on the little patio was a tall, thin man with a slightly hooked nose and sharp, intelligent eyes.

Her brow wrinkled as she stared up at him. "Sherlock?" she asked, even though she knew he wasn't the venerable detective. He looked like Holmes, but there were marked differences.

He shook his head, glancing up at the sky before his eyes captured hers again. "Don't you recognize me, daughter?"

She gasped. Although it had been years since she looked at a photograph of her father, once he pointed out his identity she instantly recognized him.

"How is this possible?" she asked. "What are you doing here?"

He ignored her questions and glanced at the sky again. Her eyes followed his gaze. The eclipse was nearly complete, the moon a giant red orb in the sky.

"The planets are nearly aligned," he told her, pointing to several of the brightest stars as well as the easily identifiable twinkling red Mars. His eyes were wide when he looked back at her. "When they all fall into place, it's going to be a helluva show."

"What does that mean?"

"Everything will change," he continued, still ignoring her question. "For the town and for you. You have to be prepared."

"Wait!" she snapped. "I don't understand anything you're saying, and even if I did, why should I believe a word you say? You abandoned me when I was just a baby? Why would I trust you?"

He knelt down next to her, shaking his head with vehemence. "I didn't abandon you. I loved your mother, and you."

"Where the hell did you go?"

"I came back to Saint's Grove to visit my sister." A hardened expression crossed his face and a muscle in his

jaw ticked. "I was a student of anthropology, you know, and whenever I came home I spent time with Professor McGurty at the college. On this occasion, he had a collection of local artifacts, one of particular interest to me. It was a strangely shaped piece of metal, dull and tarnished so I knew it was silver, and covered in strange markings. It was clearly a language of some sort, and I was excited to have the opportunity to try and decipher it. I spent hours recreating it on paper so I could study it later. When I left, a strange woman confronted me in the parking lot and then next thing I knew I was ... somewhere else."

"Somewhere else?" Irene echoed scornfully. "Where?"

He shook his head in frustration and stood up. "I don't know. Here but not here. I can move about the town sometimes, watch people, see things, but I can't interact with anyone." A worried expression swept across his face. "The world is not what it appears to be."

"What does that mean?" *Irene stressed. "And if that's all true, how can you interact with me now?"*

He pointed at the sky. "The eclipse and the planets. Everything is beginning to merge and it's going to bring chaos to Saint's Grove." He leaned down and grasped her hand. "Promise me you'll be careful."

Something in the expression on his face made her believe him and she nodded.

His face softened and he patted her hand. "Good girl." Standing he turned as though he was going to leave, but stopped and looked down at her one more time. "Irene, I'm so sorry about your mother."

A lump developed in her throat and she struggled to contain the sudden tears in her eyes. She gave him a slight nod before he turned and seemed to fade away.

"Where are you going?" she called after him. "I have so many questions for you. Wait!"

"Wait!" Irene sat up, reaching out for the man who was no longer there. It took her a moment to realize she'd been dreaming and she sat back with a sigh, wiping several tears from her cheeks.

What a strange dream.

She rarely thought about her father, let alone dreamt about him, and yet, the entire experience felt so real she struggled to believe it wasn't.

She thought about his words, his warnings about the eclipse and alignment of planets.

The eclipse!

She glanced up at the sky, realizing she'd almost forgotten about it. The moon looked bigger than she had ever seen it before, swollen and red. Her eyes picked out the brightest stars, noting that they seemed to sit in a perfect row in the sky.

There had been plenty of people in the town square before she fell asleep, but now there didn't seem to be an available square yard of lawn left.

Did all ten thousand residents come out? she thought wryly.

Suddenly, a squeal rang out from somewhere down below. "Look!" a voice called and her eyes scanned the square, trying to find the owner.

She watched as a number of people glanced up in the sky and she followed their gaze, gasping when she did so.

A shooting star streaked across the sky, followed by another, then another, leaving a trail of rainbow colors behind them. Irene stood up as the heavens seemed to fill with the meteorites, their light casting blue and pink and orange and green shadows on the people below.

She watched in awe. Never had she seen such a strange and wonderful sight.

Suddenly, a new meteorite came plummeting down from the heavens. It moved faster than the others, and she realized it was heading straight for the square.

It's going to hit, she thought with horror.

"Look out!" she shouted, pointing at it.

Several people glanced up as it came crashing down at the foot of the statue of Peter Saint, leaving a crater the size of a small car.

Screams rang out from the crowd as chaos erupted. She saw Sheriff Duvall off in the distance talking hurriedly into her radio, and the dozen or so police officers scattered around the square began trying to direct people to safety.

More meteorites touched down as people began to leap up and run for cover. Streams of light burst forth from the crater in front of the statue like giant sparks from a campfire, and Irene watched in terror as the lights shot off in random directions. She watch as the lights landed in random places, hitting buildings and people.

If she thought the scene had been chaotic before, it was nothing compared to what happened as the lights touched down.

Everything was true, she realized. Every rumor and myth and legend ever told about Saint's Grove was one hundred percent, categorically true.

Irene could only stand, watching helplessly as those struck by the lights began to transform.

She saw an average looking man with brown hair and a slight pot belly fall to the ground, writhing as though in pain as his body bubbled and grew until a gigantic snarling wolf crouched low to the ground before sprinting through the crowd towards the edge of town.

A blonde woman struck by another light suddenly sprouted enormous white feathery wings, and after a moment she leapt into the sky, the powerful wings lifting her high and carrying her away.

A bloodcurdling scream filled the night and Irene searched the crowd until she found the source; a thin woman in the grasp of a tall, pale man who ripped at her throat until her blood flowed freely. He roared in triumph as he placed his mouth over the wound, sucking ferociously at her neck and licking up every drop of blood.

At the sight of the vampire, Irene dropped to her knees, hiding behind the edge of the balcony, as she recalled the dream and her father's warning. "My God, he was right," she whispered.

The implications hit her, and she realized that it was a very real possibility that he truly hadn't abandoned her and her mother, that he really had been trapped between worlds all these years.

"My God," she whispered again, stunned.

She peeked over the edge of the balcony, watching as the lights continued to stream out of the crater. She saw the museum curators, Mark and Lisa Hunter, hurrying down the street toward their building, their matching brown hair streaming behind them as they ran.

Sophia Neilson, the bank manager, crouched down near one of the street vendor carts, her long black hair nearly covering her face.

Across the square she saw the beautiful Anika Butler leap up from a table at the coffee shop and race for her antique store, her milk chocolate skin glistening under the lights dancing in the sky.

Suddenly, another stream of light burst forth from the crater and she watched in terror as it seemed to zoom directly toward the bookstore.

She ducked back down again, screaming as the light came straight down on the store. She curled up in a ball, waiting for the house to explode around her. Several moments later when the building still stood she looked out from behind her arms.

A warm glow filled the apartment and she watched as it seemed to move downstairs toward the store. Soon, it disappeared down the stairs, fading away until it was no longer visible.

Irene hesitated for a moment. Had it somehow entered the building? Were all her precious books downstairs smoldering away as she sat, too scared to move?

Get up, she told herself fiercely. *Get up and go check. Protect what's yours.*

Climbing to her feet, albeit unsteadily, she tiptoed through the apartment, stopping only to retrieve her fire extinguisher from under the kitchen sink.

She continued down the stairs, pressing herself against the wall and holding the extinguisher in both hands like a weapon.

She reached the bottom stair and her bare foot touched the hardwood floor of at the bottom of the landing, cool on her toes.

Gulping down her fear, she crept out into the open.

The store was dark, the lights from outside casting ominous shadows that danced throughout the rooms.

A flash from outside illuminated the foyer and Irene couldn't stop the scream that tore from her throat.

Laying in the middle of the room was a very bloody and beaten, very naked and unconscious man.

CHAPTER THREE

After a moment, Irene realized the man hadn't moved an inch and her screaming subsided.

He's hurt, she realized. *Badly.*

Her fear warred with her desire to see if he needed help, and finally the latter won out and she slowly moved toward him until she stood above him, peering down.

Despite the several days' growth of beard covering his face, his handsome features were obvious. His full lips and a strong aquiline nose were framed by high cheekbones slashing across his face. A smattering of hair covered his firmly sculpted chest as well as the rest of lean hard frame. Irene flushed as she tried to avoid looking at one area in particular, but her eyes strayed for a split second and she almost dropped the fire extinguisher. Despite his injuries, he was clearly in excellent shape.

He stirred suddenly, moaning, and she took a quick step back.

"Stella," he groaned.

His heartfelt plea softened Irene, and she put down the extinguisher and dropped to her knees.

"Shh," she tried to calm him as he stirred even more.

His eyelids fluttered then opened, revealing deep chocolate brown eyes that met hers for a brief second before he lifted a hand to her cheek. "Are you an angel?" he asked hazily as a sleepy smile crossed his face. "A beautiful angel."

She blushed and shook her head. "No," she answered. "I'm Irene."

His eyes seemed to focus, narrowing as they centered on her. A moment later, his hands shot up and grabbed her by the shoulders.

She shrieked.

"Who are you?" he demanded, his eyes wild as they moved about the store. "What have you done to me?" His hands squeezed her shoulders painfully and he gave her a little shake.

She whimpered and tried to pull away. "You're hurting me." She pressed a hand against his chest, and despite the pain in her shoulder felt a small thrill when she felt his hard flesh beneath her hand.

His eyes flew back to her face and a moment later his face lost some of its hardness and he let her go. She scrambled across the floor, breathing heavily as she tried to gain control of her emotions.

"My apologies, Miss." He struggled to sit up, and in doing so, for the first time seemed to notice his nakedness.

His face flushed a brilliant red as one hand reached across his chest and the other moved to cover his groin area. "I, uh, I don't have, that is, I seem to be lacking clothes," he finished lamely.

The sight of such an impressive male specimen acting like a chaste schoolgirl suddenly seemed immensely funny to her and she barely held back her laughter.

"Just a moment," she said, her voice breaking a little as she choked back a giggle. "I'll bring you something to cover yourself."

She ran upstairs as fast as her feet could carry her, grabbing the blanket she kept on the back of her couch and was back down the stairs and at his side a moment later.

"Here," she handed him the blanket.

He wrapped it around his waist and tried to climb to his feet.

"Whoa," she reached out a hand to help steady him as he stumbled a bit. He leaned on her for a moment, looking down at her. Time seemed to stand still as his brown eyes met her green ones. A strange expression crossed his face, one she couldn't identify, but something about it pulled at the core of her and she felt herself wanting to lean into him.

The moment ended as he regained his balance and pulled away, and she stepped back as he looked around the store.

A frown creased his face. "What is going on? How did I get here? What is this place?"

"This is my bookstore. As far as how you got here," she shrugged. "I don't know. And I have no idea what happened to you. Where did you come from?"

His eyes widened as he looked at the back room and staircase. "What the devil! This is my office," he exclaimed, his eyes darting back to her with an accusing glare. "Who are you? What have you done?"

"*Your* office?" she squeaked. "I don't think so. Like I

said, this is my bookstore."

"I think not," he responded haughtily, drawing himself to his full height and pointing to the stairs. "You may have altered much of it, but I recognize my family home."

"Your family home!" she gaped. "This house has been in the Bell family for several generations."

"I think I know my own home."

"Look," she replied with a lift of her chin. "I'm not the one who was passed out naked in the middle of the floor with no idea how I got there. Clearly your memory can't be counted on right now."

He opened his mouth to reply, then closed it, frowning. "I don't understand what's happening."

"Neither do I," she answered a little more kindly. "The only thing I do know is that you're hurt." She pointed to his chest, and he looked down, seeming to notice his injuries for the first time.

"Yes, I suppose I am." His face was a mask of confusion, and Irene began to feel sorry for him.

"Come upstairs," she told him. "We'll get you cleaned up."

He looked around another moment before nodding and following her to the stairs.

"You first," she indicated. "In case you fall," she explained when he hesitated.

He looked at her doubtfully, as if questioning her ability to catch him, but climbed the stairs as indicated.

Once they reached the top, she led him to the living room. "Please make yourself at home," she told him. She dashed around the apartment gathering items to tend to his wounds, her hands shaking with nerves. She wasn't used to having anyone in her home, let alone a handsome and naked stranger. For that matter, she'd never had any naked man in her apartment.

Or your bed, she thought suddenly. She felt her face flame and pushed the thought away. After all, it never bothered her before, why would it suddenly bother her now?

When she made her way back to the living room, she found the man standing in front of the television hanging on the wall, his confused expression reflected in the black screen as he touched it, leaving obvious smudges with his fingertips. "What is this … thing?"

"Are you kidding?" she asked.

He stared at her.

"It's a flat screen TV," she answered. "What, do you still have one of those big boxy ones?"

"Tee vee?" he echoed.

Irene suddenly felt sorry for him.

Poor thing, she thought. *He must have lost his memory or something. I wonder what happened to him.*

"Come," she pointed at the couch. "We can clean up your wounds. Or would you rather take a shower first?"

He glanced outside at the dark sky. "Do you know of a bathhouse open at such a late hour?"

The dark sky, Irene realized. She walked to the doors of the balcony and looked out, realizing that the meteorite shower had ceased, and the town square while not completely empty, had cleared significantly.

Except for a number of bodies, she noted with horror. And the entire Saint's Grove police department.

There were several ambulances parked along the edge of the square, as well as a number of EMT's helping the injured. White sheets covered the dead, and there were a number of people standing along the edge of the square, many crying and holding each other.

Irene felt as though her heart would break and had to look away.

Glancing back at the injured man in her living room, she also realized that the Saint's Grove authorities would have no time to deal with him. He might have blood on him, but he seemed relatively unharmed by whatever had happened to him. Clearly, she would have to take care of him in light of everything.

At least for the night.

Realizing she could barely see him, she stepped back into the apartment and moved to turn on an end table lamp.

The light flicked on, illuminating the room, and he gasped.

"You have electric lights!" he exclaimed, looking at her with new interest. "You must be quite wealthy. I've only heard of them being used in cities, and even then, only by the most well-to-do."

She snorted. "Hardly. I make enough to pay the bills, but I'm still waiting for the day I can take that European vacation I've always dreamed of."

His brow wrinkled as he looked up at her.

She stared back for a moment. "Would you like to take that shower now?"

He looked around the room, his face growing more and more confused until he finally looked up at her again. "Please," he stressed. "Can you tell me *what is going on*?"

Irene thought about the eclipse and the alignment of the planets, as well her father appearing in her dream.

Perhaps not a dream. Perhaps he really was there, just on some other plane of existence. She'd never believed in such things, but after watching the events that had just unfolded in the town square, she clearly didn't know as much about the world as she thought.

"I don't know," she told him honestly. "All I know is that I was watching a lunar eclipse on my balcony," she pointed toward the double doors leading to it. "Along with the rest of Saint's Grove when a bunch of meteorites hit the town square and all hell broke loose. There were … things," she finished awkwardly.

He stood and hurried to the doors, bursting through them to stare down on the square. "My God," he breathed.

Irene moved to stand next to him, looking down on the scene below.

"What are those contraptions?" he asked, pointing at an ambulance as two EMT's loaded a gurney into it.

She stared at him again. "Ambulances."

"What is going on? What has happened to the square?" He gasped as the EMT's climbed inside the cab and drove off. Gulping, he looked at her with wide eyes. "What kind of magic is this?" he breathed.

Irene stared at him. She'd had a nagging sensation tickling at the back of her brain ever since he claimed to be in his office downstairs.

"What is your name?" she asked. "Where are you from?"

"Here," he exclaimed. "I'm from here. Saint's Grove." He looked down again and pointed to the statue of Peter Saint. "That statue has been standing in that very spot my entire life. I grew up playing in the square. But that …"

He shook his head with vehemence. "That is not the town I grew up in. things are the same but different. Everything is changed." He looked down on her and once again gripped her shoulders in his strong hands and stared down at her with a plaintive vehemence. *"Please,"* he begged. "Tell me what is going on."

His eyes seemed to pool as she looked up at him and she felt herself trying to resist melting into him. "I don't know," she answered honestly. "All I know is something happened when the meteorite hit the square. I saw things that only exist in fairy tales. And then you showed up in my store." She thought about her dream, what her father told her about existing in another reality. As she stared at the man holding her, a new thought occurred to her. "What's the last thing you remember? Take a deep breath and think hard."

He let go of her and closed his eyes, breathing in long and steady. "I was working. The weather was cold outside, windy, and I built a fire in the office for the warmth as well as the light. Stella came unexpectedly, and we talked about the Hawkins case. Several men burst in, and ..." he trailed off as his eyes popped opened and a mix of fear and anger shadowed his face. "One of them stabbed me!"

His hands dropped to his chest, followed by his eyes as he searched his wounds. "He stabbed me in the chest, why is there no wound?" Looking back up at her, he gripped her shoulders again. "Did you do this? Did you heal me somehow?"

"No," she shook her head. "I found you in the store, hurt and unconscious." She was finally beginning to calm down a bit from her earlier shock of the meteorites and the strange creatures she'd seen. There were still many unanswered questions, but rushing about in a panic wouldn't help anything.

After all, what would Holmes do? Panic like a silly ninny, or try to look at the situation objectively.

"Be steady, Miss Bell," he would tell her. "Never forget that we must delve deep until we find the truth. It is a process of elimination, my dear. If you've eliminated all other possibilities whatever remains must be the truth."

"Yes, Mr. Holmes," she muttered.

"Who is Mr. Holmes?" the man holding her asked.

Irene felt her face flame. *Did I say that out loud?*

She didn't answer the question. Instead, keeping the memory of her father and her dream that was not a dream fresh, she asked, "I know this seems like a strange and unusual question, but tell me, what year is it?"

"It is the year of our Lord, one thousand eight hundred Seventy-five."

"1875," she breathed. "Tell me, *what is your name?*"

He had sharp eyes, a sign of a keen intellect, she realized.

"My name is Benjamin Churchill."

"Benjamin, my name is Irene Bell," she told him. "And it might have been 1875 when you were here, but from my perspective it's 2016."

CHAPTER FOUR

He pushed Irene's hand off his shoulder and stood. "I don't understand what is happening to me, but I am clearly not dead." One hand slammed down on his chest. "I am flesh and blood, and you madam," he pointed at her, "Are a trickster or a witch and I will not listen to anymore lies. It is time you left my house."

With that, he scooped her up off the couch and threw her over his shoulder.

Irene shrieked, struggling to get away. He clamped a strong arm down across her legs. "Who do you think you are?" she yelled. "Put me down!"

He ignored her, hurrying down the stairs, across the store and threw open the front door, and started to drop her on the porch.

Realizing his intent, Irene fought to stay in the house. "I don't know what the hell you think you're doing, but if you don't let me in my house *right now*, I'll call the police."

"Please do," he stared down at her. "I'd be happy to discuss your nefarious deeds with them. In fact, I believe I'll call your bluff and fetch them myself." He stepped out of the front door, strode across the front porch and down the stairs.

As soon as his foot hit the grass in front of the house, he swayed. Turning to look at her he hissed, "what spell is this?"

"Benjamin," she gasped. "What is happening to you?"

He seemed to fade right before her eyes, his body turning translucent under the moonlight, paling until he looked like the gray after-image of a photograph.

He groaned and put a hand up to touch his face, but as his fingers swept across the place where his cheek would be, they grasped only air, passing straight through his face.

He opened his mouth to speak, but no sound came out. He looked at her, his expression wild with fear.

"Benjamin," she whispered, reaching out a hand. "Please. Come back inside."

His strength seemed to fade along with his body and he staggered forward until he fell, landing on the porch. He collapsed, his face against the white boards.

Irene was at his side in a flash, her hand on his shoulder as his body seemed to regain its form.

He gasped, his chest heaving as he breathed.

"Oh, Benjamin." Irene gathered him in her arms. "Please trust me. I don't know what the hell is going on, but I promise you I'll help you find out."

He turned in her arms, his hands gripping her shoulders as he studied her face. Finally, he nodded and she felt him relax in her arms.

"He's dead," came a voice.

Irene looked up to see Flora, one of the local palm readers. Irene had never given much stock to such things as palm reading, but now, looking at the slender woman, she wondered how she could have been so foolish. Flora rarely came to town and usually seemed unobtrusive and reserved, but not now. She wore what looked like a flowery silk muumuu and her short blonde hair ruffled in the wind. The reddish brown shadow of the waning eclipse casting a strange pall over her weathered face, giving her an ethereal appearance, and Irene wondered how she'd never noticed the quiet power in the other woman.

"What?" Benjamin struggled to sit up, his voice raspy and faint. "What did you say?"

Flora's blue eyes were filled with sorrow when she looked at him. "You're dead. You died in this house and you never crossed over. That's why you're here now. The planets aligned at the same time as the eclipse and it ripped a hole between worlds, allowing you to come back as you were. But only in this house." She pointed at the bookstore.

"Dead?" Irene squeaked.

Flora grinned. "Yes. A ghost. That's why he can't leave, why he can't maintain his corporeal form outside the house. He's tied to it."

Benjamin glared at her. "Are you a witch?"

She smiled. "Yes."

He hissed, pulling away from Irene and moved backward on the porch until he was pressed against the front door. "Stay away from me."

Her smile softened a little. "I'm not going to hurt you.

I'm a good witch."

Benjamin snorted. "Is there any such thing?"

She took a step forward. "Of course. As with any profession, there are good and bad. Light and dark. Dark witches call on powers that conflict with nature. Good witches practice magic in accordance with Mother Earth and accept what is."

Benjamin snorted again, his derision obvious, but Irene ignored him and stood up.

"So what do we do?" she asked. "Can you help him?"

Flora's smile fled and her eyes seemed to fill with tears, shimmering in the strange light. "Maybe. I don't know. As I said before, the eclipse tore a hole between worlds. He's only here now because he didn't cross over."

"You keep saying that," Irene frowned. "Are you saying there really is a heaven?"

Flora laughed. "Heaven, Valhalla, Paradise, Tir Na Nog, Nirvana, the Afterlife, whatever you call it, it is still the same. It is still the place you go when you pass from this existence into the next." She made a sweeping gesture with one arm.

Benjamin's spoke, his voice still hoarse but growing stronger, and both women turned to look at him. "If what you say is true, how do I cross over?"

She studied him for a moment. "I sense a curse on you."

"A curse?" Irene repeated weakly.

The older woman nodded. "Yes. It is the reason he didn't cross over. Cursed souls cannot enter the other realm."

Benjamin pushed himself to a sitting position. "Is there a way to break the curse?"

"You must first find out who cursed you and how." She glanced at the sky. "And you must do it soon. The rift between worlds won't stay open forever. Once it closes, you'll be trapped again until the next time the planets align in conjunction with the blood moon."

Irene frowned. "How long do we have?"

"Magic is wild and sometimes unpredictable, but there is still order to it," Flora told them, her eyes closing. Her head fell back and she seemed to enter an almost dream-like state. "The moon is inextricably linked to the number seven. When the moon reaches its apex on the seventh night, the rifts will seal themselves and all will be as it was." Her eyes popped open. "You have one week."

Irene felt all the blood drain from her face as she looked at Benjamin. Something inside her ached and she suddenly felt like crying. Benjamin stared back at her and for a moment she was certain he felt the same way.

"One week," he murmured. "That's not much time."

Bereft, Irene sat down on the top step of the porch. "You said he'd be trapped until the next time this," she waved a hand at the sky, "thing happens. When will that be?"

Flora glanced at the grass in front of the house, and it seemed she refused to meet their gaze. "It is a rare occurrence. Once maybe every thousand years."

Irene gasped, her eyes flying to Benjamin who wore the same expression of horror she felt. "A thousand years," she breathed.

Benjamin climbed to his feet, stumbling a little and Irene quickly stood, stepping to his side to offer a hand of support.

He looked out at the diminutive witch. "How on earth

do I go about breaking a curse put on me over one hundred years ago?"

She pursed her lips, thinking, before she answered slowly, drawing each word out as if she was carefully choosing each one. "Do you know how you died?"

Benjamin nodded, running a hand through his shaggy hair. "I believe I do. I was stabbed. Murdered."

"Stabbed," Flora breathed as her eyes widened. "Do you recall the weapon? Can you describe it?"

He frowned. "I think so. It was a knife, of course. A strange looking piece. The handle seemed to be made of silver. A very odd shape with strange markings."

His words stirred a memory in Irene, and her mind flashed to the words her father had spoken in her dream earlier. *It was a strangely shaped piece of metal, dull and tarnished so I knew it was silver, and covered in strange markings.* She started to open her mouth to tell the others about the strange coincidence, but Flora spoke first.

"The Star Anthame," she gasped. "I knew it."

Benjamin's brow wrinkled. "Star Anthame?" he repeated. "Pray tell, what on earth is that?"

"The Star Anthame was an ancient weapon, forged by a coven who gave it the power to be wielded only by our kind. Witches, that is. Though it could not be used to kill, it could be graced with a witch's power and used to curse the person it was used against. That is why you didn't cross over, why you have lingered in limbo instead of truly dying." She shook her head, frowning. "Unfortunately …"

"What?" Benjamin glared at her.

Flora gave him a sad look. "Unfortunately it fell into the wrong hands at one point. Worse, it was a witch. She began using black magic, growing more and more powerful until she possessed the power to jump from body to body, thereby allowing her to live forever. She has gone by many names." She shook her head. "If she used the blade against you, it was because you must have gotten in her way."

"Where is this Star An- Anth- whatever," Irene stuttered. "Where is it now? Can we use it to break the curse?"

"Possibly. However," Flora looked at the ground. "It was destroyed."

Irene gaped. "Destroyed?"

"Yes," the small witch nodded. "Sometime around 1883 the local coven was able to steal it back from the witch, known as Edith at that time. It was broken into three pieces. The blade, the hilt, and the gemstone. Where they are now, I can only guess. No one knows."

All the color drained from Benjamin's face, and for a moment, he looked as though he might faint. When he spoke, his voice was almost a whisper. "Surely there is some other way to break the curse."

"There is one thing," Flora offered. "As a magical piece it is bound to its place of origin. Somehow, they always find their way home. I believe they are here, in Saint's Grove, somewhere. If you can find them and assemble them, I may be able to help you break the curse."

"Is that the only way?" Irene asked.

"Perhaps not," Flora answered. "But it is the only way I know."

She glanced at the town square, then the sky. "I have to go now. I must be getting home. Come see me when you find the relics."

"How will we know what they look like?" Benjamin asked.

"You've already seen it," Flora answered as she walked away. "Remember."

Irene watched for a moment as the other woman moved further and further away, then turned back to Benjamin.

"Let's go back inside," she told him.

He seemed to have lost all suspicion of her and nodded in agreement, taking her elbow in one hand as he opened the door for her.

"Irene." She stopped in the foyer to look up at him, a strange twinge pulling at her chest as she took in his somber expression. "I am terribly ashamed of my rough treatment of you earlier. You've been nothing but kind to me since I awoke, and I have rewarded you with suspicion and violence. Can you forgive me?"

His eyes bore into her and she felt her entire body flush. It was all she could do to stop herself from melting into him. "There's nothing to forgive," she breathed. "I would have probably reacted the same way. You've been through a horrible experience."

He smiled, his eyes crinkling slightly at the edges, and she almost swooned.

"As I cannot leave the store, I will continue to need your help," he said, his voice soft. "Will you help me look for the Star Anthame? And try to discover the fate of my brother as well as Stella?"

Irene felt as if someone had thrown a glass of ice water in her face. His fiancée. She kept forgetting about her. She pushed away the tiny streak of resentment that coursed through her. "Yes, I'll help you. I'm not sure how, but I will do what I can."

She nodded. "But not tonight. I'm exhausted, and I'm

sure you are too. We should get some sleep before we do anything else."

He agreed and followed her upstairs to the apartment.

What will I do? She thought. *I don't even know where to start. How on earth am I going to help him?*

It's elementary, my dear Miss Bell, rang a familiar voice in Irene's head. *You must simply focus. Use your keen intellect and powers of observation. I am certain you will ascertain the truth.*

For the first time in her life, she found herself getting mad at Holmes. She shook her head a little, balling her hands into fists. "Just shut up," she muttered.

"What?"

Irene flushed and her face felt so hot she was certain she could set fires with it. Did she really talk out loud to Holmes that often?

"Nothing," she answered lamely as they entered her living room.

"Do you always speak to yourself in that manner?"

She glanced at him. His eyes sparkled a tiny smile quirking one side of his mouth, and she realized he was teasing her.

She laughed softly as she led him to the tiny spare room tucked under the arch of the house. "Apparently I do. At least, when I'm around you."

She opened the door to the spare room. A single bed was pushed against the wall under the arch, and a small desk and two drawer filing cabinet sat against the opposite wall. "You can sleep here," she told him. "I know it's small, but it's all I have unless you want to sleep on the couch."

She opened a microscopic closet on one side of the

door and pointed to the high shelf. "There are extra blankets and pillows if you need them."

"Thank you."

She turned and looked at him, suddenly feeling nervous and awkward. "Do you need anything else? A toothbrush, maybe a cup of tea?"

He shook his head, and they stood in silence, staring at each other.

"I should let you get to sleep," she breathed, not moving an inch.

He nodded, still silent, and a moment later he reached across the space between them.

Irene stifled a gasp as his fingers gently swept a wisp of hair off her face and tucked it behind her ear.

"Thank you for your kindness," he whispered, his fingers lingering. One seemed to caress the spot just behind her ear so softly she wasn't completely sure it had happened.

It didn't matter. This time Irene couldn't stop herself and she shuddered slightly at the very thought of him touching her in such a way.

As soon as she did, however, he dropped his hand and stepped back.

"Good- good night," she stammered and fled the room.

She escaped to her bedroom as fast as her feet would take her, leaning against the door once it was shut. Taking several deep breaths, she attempted to calm her senses.

"What is going on?" she whispered to herself.

It's patently obvious, came the voice of a disappointed Holmes. *You have surrendered to the basest human emotion, my dear Miss Bell; lust.*

"Lust? I don't think so," she lied.

Miss Bell, he replied with a pitying tone. *You may be able to hide your reactions from everyone else, but I am trained to observe the nuances and details that no one else can see. Additionally, who knows you better than I?*

Irene felt herself growing supremely irritated with him. "Shut up!" she snapped. "I don't care what you say, I'm just trying to help the guy. Besides, he a *ghost*! That's like, like, weird. And anyway, he'll be gone in a week. It'd be stupid to fall for a man like that."

Are you attempting to convince me? Or yourself?

She straightened, storming across the room and yanking her pajamas out of a drawer. "Go away," she snarled as she changed into silky pink shorts and matching tank top.

Her nightclothes were one of the few concessions she made to her femininity. Unlike her jeans and bulky sweaters, no one saw her in them, she liked the feel of silk and satin on her skin, and just like most women, she actually liked to feel girly at least once in a while.

She breathed a sigh of relief when no response came from Holmes and climbed into bed.

Her eyes grew heavy the moment her head hit the pillow. "Maybe I'll wake up in the morning and discover this was all a bad dream," she mumbled.

But as she drifted off, she knew no such thing would happen. For better or worse, Benjamin was here, stuck in her bookstore and she was the only person who could help him.

CHAPTER FIVE

H e pushed Irene's hand off his shoulder and stood. "I don't understand what is happening to me, but I am clearly not dead." One hand slammed down on his chest. "I am flesh and blood, and you madam," he pointed at her, "Are a trickster or a witch and I will not listen to anymore lies. It is time you left my house."

With that, he scooped her up off the couch and threw her over his shoulder.

Irene shrieked, struggling to get away. He clamped a strong arm down across her legs. "Who do you think you are?" she yelled. "Put me down!"

He ignored her, hurrying down the stairs, across the store and threw open the front door, and started to drop her on the porch.

Realizing his intent, Irene fought to stay in the house. "I don't know what the hell you think you're doing, but if you don't let me in my house *right now*, I'll call the police."

"Please do," he stared down at her. "I'd be happy to discuss your nefarious deeds with them. In fact, I believe I'll call your bluff and fetch them myself." He stepped out of the front door, strode across the front porch and down the stairs.

As soon as his foot hit the grass in front of the house, he swayed. Turning to look at her he hissed, "what spell is this?"

"Benjamin," she gasped. "What is happening to you?"

He seemed to fade right before her eyes, his body turning translucent under the moonlight, paling until he looked like the gray after-image of a photograph.

He groaned and put a hand up to touch his face, but as his fingers swept across the place where his cheek would be, they grasped only air, passing straight through his face.

He opened his mouth to speak, but no sound came out. He looked at her, his expression wild with fear.

"Benjamin," she whispered, reaching out a hand. "Please. Come back inside."

His strength seemed to fade along with his body and he staggered forward until he fell, landing on the porch. He collapsed, his face against the white boards.

Irene was at his side in a flash, her hand on his shoulder as his body seemed to regain its form.

He gasped, his chest heaving as he breathed.

"Oh, Benjamin." Irene gathered him in her arms. "Please trust me. I don't know what the hell is going on, but I promise you I'll help you find out."

He turned in her arms, his hands gripping her shoulders as he studied her face. Finally, he nodded and she felt him relax in her arms.

"He's dead," came a voice.

Irene looked up to see Flora, one of the local palm readers. Irene had never given much stock to such things as palm reading, but now, looking at the slender woman, she wondered how she could have been so foolish. Flora rarely came to town and usually seemed unobtrusive and reserved, but not now. She wore what looked like a flowery silk muumuu and her short blonde hair ruffled in the wind. The reddish brown shadow of the waning eclipse casting a strange pall over her weathered face, giving her an ethereal appearance, and Irene wondered how she'd never noticed the quiet power in the other woman.

"What?" Benjamin struggled to sit up, his voice raspy and faint. "What did you say?"

Flora's blue eyes were filled with sorrow when she looked at him. "You're dead. You died in this house and you never crossed over. That's why you're here now. The planets aligned at the same time as the eclipse and it ripped a hole between worlds, allowing you to come back as you were. But only in this house." She pointed at the bookstore.

"Dead?" Irene squeaked.

Flora grinned. "Yes. A ghost. That's why he can't leave, why he can't maintain his corporeal form outside the house. He's tied to it."

Benjamin glared at her. "Are you a witch?"

She smiled. "Yes."

He hissed, pulling away from Irene and moved backward on the porch until he was pressed against the front door. "Stay away from me."

Her smile softened a little. "I'm not going to hurt you.

I'm a good witch."

Benjamin snorted. "Is there any such thing?"

She took a step forward. "Of course. As with any profession, there are good and bad. Light and dark. Dark witches call on powers that conflict with nature. Good witches practice magic in accordance with Mother Earth and accept what is."

Benjamin snorted again, his derision obvious, but Irene ignored him and stood up.

"So what do we do?" she asked. "Can you help him?"

Flora's smile fled and her eyes seemed to fill with tears, shimmering in the strange light. "Maybe. I don't know. As I said before, the eclipse tore a hole between worlds. He's only here now because he didn't cross over."

"You keep saying that," Irene frowned. "Are you saying there really is a heaven?"

Flora laughed. "Heaven, Valhalla, Paradise, Tir Na Nog, Nirvana, the Afterlife, whatever you call it, it is still the same. It is still the place you go when you pass from this existence into the next." She made a sweeping gesture with one arm.

Benjamin's spoke, his voice still hoarse but growing stronger, and both women turned to look at him. "If what you say is true, how do I cross over?"

She studied him for a moment. "I sense a curse on you."

"A curse?" Irene repeated weakly.

The older woman nodded. "Yes. It is the reason he didn't cross over. Cursed souls cannot enter the other realm."

Benjamin pushed himself to a sitting position. "Is there a way to break the curse?"

"You must first find out who cursed you and how." She glanced at the sky. "And you must do it soon. The rift between worlds won't stay open forever. Once it closes, you'll be trapped again until the next time the planets align in conjunction with the blood moon."

Irene frowned. "How long do we have?"

"Magic is wild and sometimes unpredictable, but there is still order to it," Flora told them, her eyes closing. Her head fell back and she seemed to enter an almost dream-like state. "The moon is inextricably linked to the number seven. When the moon reaches its apex on the seventh night, the rifts will seal themselves and all will be as it was." Her eyes popped open. "You have one week."

Irene felt all the blood drain from her face as she looked at Benjamin. Something inside her ached and she suddenly felt like crying. Benjamin stared back at her and for a moment she was certain he felt the same way.

"One week," he murmured. "That's not much time."

Bereft, Irene sat down on the top step of the porch. "You said he'd be trapped until the next time this," she waved a hand at the sky, "thing happens. When will that be?"

Flora glanced at the grass in front of the house, and it seemed she refused to meet their gaze. "It is a rare occurrence. Once maybe every thousand years."

Irene gasped, her eyes flying to Benjamin who wore the same expression of horror she felt. "A thousand years," she breathed.

Benjamin climbed to his feet, stumbling a little and Irene quickly stood, stepping to his side to offer a hand of support.

He looked out at the diminutive witch. "How on earth

do I go about breaking a curse put on me over one hundred years ago?"

She pursed her lips, thinking, before she answered slowly, drawing each word out as if she was carefully choosing each one. "Do you know how you died?"

Benjamin nodded, running a hand through his shaggy hair. "I believe I do. I was stabbed. Murdered."

"Stabbed," Flora breathed as her eyes widened. "Do you recall the weapon? Can you describe it?"

He frowned. "I think so. It was a knife, of course. A strange looking piece. The handle seemed to be made of silver. A very odd shape with strange markings."

His words stirred a memory in Irene, and her mind flashed to the words her father had spoken in her dream earlier. *It was a strangely shaped piece of metal, dull and tarnished so I knew it was silver, and covered in strange markings.* She started to open her mouth to tell the others about the strange coincidence, but Flora spoke first.

"The Star Anthame," she gasped. "I knew it."

Benjamin's brow wrinkled. "Star Anthame?" he repeated. "Pray tell, what on earth is that?"

"The Star Anthame was an ancient weapon, forged by a coven who gave it the power to be wielded only by our kind. Witches, that is. Though it could not be used to kill, it could be graced with a witch's power and used to curse the person it was used against. That is why you didn't cross over, why you have lingered in limbo instead of truly dying." She shook her head, frowning. "Unfortunately ..."

"What?" Benjamin glared at her.

Flora gave him a sad look. "Unfortunately it fell into the wrong hands at one point. Worse, it was a witch. She began using black magic, growing more and more powerful until she possessed the power to jump from body to body, thereby allowing her to live forever. She has gone by many names." She shook her head. "If she used the blade against you, it was because you must have gotten in her way."

"Where is this Star An- Anth- whatever," Irene stuttered. "Where is it now? Can we use it to break the curse?"

"Possibly. However," Flora looked at the ground. "It was destroyed."

Irene gaped. "Destroyed?"

"Yes," the small witch nodded. "Sometime around 1883 the local coven was able to steal it back from the witch, known as Edith at that time. It was broken into three pieces. The blade, the hilt, and the gemstone. Where they are now, I can only guess. No one knows."

All the color drained from Benjamin's face, and for a moment, he looked as though he might faint. When he spoke, his voice was almost a whisper. "Surely there is some other way to break the curse."

"There is one thing," Flora offered. "As a magical piece it is bound to its place of origin. Somehow, they always find their way home. I believe they are here, in Saint's Grove, somewhere. If you can find them and assemble them, I may be able to help you break the curse."

"Is that the only way?" Irene asked.

"Perhaps not," Flora answered. "But it is the only way I know."

She glanced at the town square, then the sky. "I have to go now. I must be getting home. Come see me when you find the relics."

"How will we know what they look like?" Benjamin asked.

"You've already seen it," Flora answered as she walked away. "Remember."

Irene watched for a moment as the other woman moved further and further away, then turned back to Benjamin.

"Let's go back inside," she told him.

He seemed to have lost all suspicion of her and nodded in agreement, taking her elbow in one hand as he opened the door for her.

"Irene." She stopped in the foyer to look up at him, a strange twinge pulling at her chest as she took in his somber expression. "I am terribly ashamed of my rough treatment of you earlier. You've been nothing but kind to me since I awoke, and I have rewarded you with suspicion and violence. Can you forgive me?"

His eyes bore into her and she felt her entire body flush. It was all she could do to stop herself from melting into him. "There's nothing to forgive," she breathed. "I would have probably reacted the same way. You've been through a horrible experience."

He smiled, his eyes crinkling slightly at the edges, and she almost swooned.

"As I cannot leave the store, I will continue to need your help," he said, his voice soft. "Will you help me look for the Star Anthame? And try to discover the fate of my brother as well as Stella?"

Irene felt as if someone had thrown a glass of ice water in her face. His fiancée. She kept forgetting about her. She pushed away the tiny streak of resentment that coursed through her. "Yes, I'll help you. I'm not sure how, but I will do what I can."

She nodded. "But not tonight. I'm exhausted, and I'm

sure you are too. We should get some sleep before we do anything else."

He agreed and followed her upstairs to the apartment.

What will I do? She thought. *I don't even know where to start. How on earth am I going to help him?*

It's elementary, my dear Miss Bell, rang a familiar voice in Irene's head. *You must simply focus. Use your keen intellect and powers of observation. I am certain you will ascertain the truth.*

For the first time in her life, she found herself getting mad at Holmes. She shook her head a little, balling her hands into fists. "Just shut up," she muttered.

"What?"

Irene flushed and her face felt so hot she was certain she could set fires with it. Did she really talk out loud to Holmes that often?

"Nothing," she answered lamely as they entered her living room.

"Do you always speak to yourself in that manner?"

She glanced at him. His eyes sparkled a tiny smile quirking one side of his mouth, and she realized he was teasing her.

She laughed softly as she led him to the tiny spare room tucked under the arch of the house. "Apparently I do. At least, when I'm around you."

She opened the door to the spare room. A single bed was pushed against the wall under the arch, and a small desk and two drawer filing cabinet sat against the opposite wall. "You can sleep here," she told him. "I know it's small, but it's all I have unless you want to sleep on the couch."

She opened a microscopic closet on one side of the

door and pointed to the high shelf. "There are extra blankets and pillows if you need them."

"Thank you."

She turned and looked at him, suddenly feeling nervous and awkward. "Do you need anything else? A toothbrush, maybe a cup of tea?"

He shook his head, and they stood in silence, staring at each other.

"I should let you get to sleep," she breathed, not moving an inch.

He nodded, still silent, and a moment later he reached across the space between them.

Irene stifled a gasp as his fingers gently swept a wisp of hair off her face and tucked it behind her ear.

"Thank you for your kindness," he whispered, his fingers lingering. One seemed to caress the spot just behind her ear so softly she wasn't completely sure it had happened.

It didn't matter. This time Irene couldn't stop herself and she shuddered slightly at the very thought of him touching her in such a way.

As soon as she did, however, he dropped his hand and stepped back.

"Good- good night," she stammered and fled the room.

She escaped to her bedroom as fast as her feet would take her, leaning against the door once it was shut. Taking several deep breaths, she attempted to calm her senses.

"What is going on?" she whispered to herself.

It's patently obvious, came the voice of a disappointed Holmes. *You have surrendered to the basest human emotion, my dear Miss Bell; lust.*

"Lust? I don't think so," she lied.

Miss Bell, he replied with a pitying tone. *You may be able to hide your reactions from everyone else, but I am trained to observe the nuances and details that no one else can see. Additionally, who knows you better than I?*

Irene felt herself growing supremely irritated with him. "Shut up!" she snapped. "I don't care what you say, I'm just trying to help the guy. Besides, he a *ghost*! That's like, like, weird. And anyway, he'll be gone in a week. It'd be stupid to fall for a man like that."

Are you attempting to convince me? Or yourself?

She straightened, storming across the room and yanking her pajamas out of a drawer. "Go away," she snarled as she changed into silky pink shorts and matching tank top.

Her nightclothes were one of the few concessions she made to her femininity. Unlike her jeans and bulky sweaters, no one saw her in them, she liked the feel of silk and satin on her skin, and just like most women, she actually liked to feel girly at least once in a while.

She breathed a sigh of relief when no response came from Holmes and climbed into bed.

Her eyes grew heavy the moment her head hit the pillow. "Maybe I'll wake up in the morning and discover this was all a bad dream," she mumbled.

But as she drifted off, she knew no such thing would happen. For better or worse, Benjamin was here, stuck in her bookstore and she was the only person who could help him.

CHAPTER SIX

Day Two

"*Irene.*"

She opened her eyes to see her father standing above her again, his lanky frame giving him an awkward appearance, something like a hovering vulture, although there was nothing menacing in his stance.

Any semblance of sleep fled and she sat up. "You were right." She grasped his hand with urgency. "I thought I was dreaming earlier, but the things I've seen." She shuddered a little.

He sat next to her, gathering her against him. The weight of his arm around her shoulders was comforting, and she leaned into him.

"I know what a shock this must all be." He squeezed

her a little. "But I'm here to help you. Here," he handed her a piece of paper folded in half.

She opened it and looked at it a moment before her eyes flew to his face. "Is this what I think it is? The Star Anthame?"

He nodded. "That's the missing word! Anthame. It was the only word that didn't make sense. I knew the artifact had something to do with the witch who sent me here. She knew I would eventually translate the writing on it, so she sent me to this dream world. I'm something of a linguist," he told her, his chest swelling slightly with pride. "She was right. I had nothing else to do but work on it all these years."

Irene's eyes widened. "What does it say?"

"Write it down," he told her. "So you don't forget when you wake up."

She scrambled for a pen from her bedside and wrote beneath the drawing as he translated for her.

"Only when the planets align and one pure heart takes another with the blade will the power of the Star Anthame be broken."

Irene finished writing it down and stared at the words. "What does it mean?"

He shook his head. "That, I don't know. Obviously it has something to do with what's going on right now, the alignment of the planets, but the rest of it? You got me."

Irene slowly read it out loud. "One pure hear takes another with the blade." Her lips clamped together. "I don't understand."

"You'll figure it out," he father told her with confidence, tapping the side of her forehead. "Just use your powers of deduction."

She grinned up at him and held up the piece of paper. "Thank you for this. It's extremely helpful."

He nodded, his face softening. "I would do anything for you," he whispered, pressing his lips against her cheek.

Irene felt tears rising in her eyes.

He gave her one last squeeze. "Wake up, my dear."

Irene opened her eyes and peered through a curtain of black hair to see the sun just beginning to peek through her window. Glancing at her alarm clock, she saw that it was five a.m. Groaning, she knew she was awake for the day. She started to push her blanket away when her hand touched something under the sheets and even before she threw the covers back she knew what she would find.

It was the drawing her father had given her.

She stared at the drawing, studying the markings as she slowly read the words she'd written aloud. "Only when the planets align and one pure heart takes another with the blade will the power of the Star Anthame be broken."

"I have to show this to Benjamin," she whispered to herself and leapt out of bed, racing through the apartment.

She reached the closed door of the guest room and stopped, hesitating for a moment. He'd had a traumatic night, perhaps she should let him sleep as long as possible.

Then Flora's words from the previous evening flooded her mind.

The moon is inextricably linked to the number seven. When the moon reaches its apex on the seventh night, the rifts will seal themselves and all will be as it was. You have one week.

"No." She shook her head, her mess of curls swinging gently around her face. "No time for that."

She gave the door a gentle rap, waiting a moment until she heard Benjamin's voice, muffled, through the peach-painted wood. "Yes?"

"Can I come in?"

She heard movement, then a moment later, "please do."

She opened the door and started to cross the room, holding out the piece of paper in front of her. "I know this is going to sound completely insane, but-" *Wham!*

In her haste, she failed to duck for the slanted ceiling and walked right into it.

Her forehead hit the ceiling with enough force to knock her off her feet. She hit the floor, landing on her back and as her vision blackened, for a moment she thought she would pass out.

"Irene!" Benjamin's voice seemed to come from far away.

"Ouch," she replied weakly.

She felt strong arms wrap around her, lifting her gently off the floor then placing her on the bed. His arms stayed around her as her vision cleared, and when it cleared enough, she saw Benjamin's concerned face peering down at her.

"Are you gravely injured?" he asked, his brow furrowing. "How may I assist?"

Pinpoints of light danced in front of her eyes as she

stared up at him.

"Ice," she managed. "Ice pack. In the freezer."

"What?"

"The big box in the kitchen," she whispered. "Top cupboard. Says ice pack right on it. Wrap it in a towel."

He got up and left the room and she relaxed, closing her eyes. Her head throbbed hotly, pulsing like a beating heart.

A moment later, she felt his arms gather her up again as a cool cloth pressed gently against her forehead.

"Ahh," she sighed.

"Better?" he asked.

"Mm-hm."

"Good."

As the throbbing in her head subsided, she became aware that Benjamin still held her. She could feel the heat of his body against her, and when she opened her eyes, she found him studying her, his eyes stormy.

Suddenly, the pain in her head seemed to vanish and she swallowed hard.

"What are you wearing?" he whispered.

Her cheeks flamed as she realized she still wore the silky shorts and tank top she'd put on the night before, which amounted to next to nothing. Suddenly, she felt exposed. Her cleavage seemed more obvious, while her shorts accentuated her soft curves more than she thought possible.

Worse, Benjamin came from a time when women were more ... discreet. What must he be thinking?

When she opened her mouth to answer, all that came out was a hoarse whisper. "Pajamas."

Fire danced in his eyes and his arms tightened around

her so slightly she wondered if she'd imagined it. "Pajamas?" he echoed, his voice husky with incredulity. "Never in my years have I seen pajamas such as this."

"All the girls wear pajamas like this," she explained weakly.

His eyes traveled down her length, pausing for a moment at the expanse of her thigh, then at the lush curves of her breasts before meeting her gaze again. His nostrils flared slightly. "I highly doubt that," he uttered hoarsely. "I cannot imagine a woman wearing them such as you do."

She blushed as her heart beat wildly at his implication. For one insane moment, she fought the urge to pull him down to her and kiss him.

Don't be ridiculous, Miss Bell, came the ever present Holmes, and she flushed. *Do what you came in here for. Give him the paper.*

She tried to ignore the tattoo of her heart and complied, holding it up. "My father came to me in a dream and gave me this," she managed to whisper.

Benjamin took the paper with one hand, still holding her with the other. After a single glance, his eyes flew back to her. "This is the knife. The one those men used to stab me. Where did you get this?"

She tried to sit up, but her vision began to swim and she laid back down. "I told you, my father. He came to me in a dream."

One of Benjamin's eyebrows shot up, and there was no mistaking the incredulity on his face as he let go of her. "Dreams aren't real, however this paper certainly is."

She felt her face grow hot with irritation and struggled into a sitting position despite her aching head. "Ghosts aren't real either," she retorted.

He opened his mouth to respond, then closed it quickly. "Yes, well," he muttered. "I suppose I must accept that the world is not what I thought it was. If I can die and come to life again in this strange new world, who am I to say your dreams are not real?"

Irene pressed her lips together as her frustration grew. "Like I said, I know it sounds crazy, but my father really did come to me in a dream. Twice now. The first time he warned me about the event, told me all sorts of things were going to happen when the eclipse came. The second time, *last night*," she stressed, "he gave me this drawing. He mentioned the artifact in the first dream, but of course I didn't connect that to you until he gave it to me. He also interpreted the markings on it." She pointed to the phrase she'd written on the bottom of the paper.

He looked at it, reading aloud. "Only when the planets align and one pure heart takes another with the blade will the power of the Star Anthame be broken." His brow furrowed. "What does it mean?"

She shrugged. "I don't know. I was thinking of asking the witch."

Benjamin nodded. "Yes, an excellent idea. If this is genuine, she will be able to tell us."

Irene stood carefully, making sure to avoid the slanted ceiling. "I'll go after breakfast. Are you hungry?"

He nodded. "Famished. Do you have more of that delectable tuna salad?"

Irene couldn't stop the grin that crossed her face. "You want tuna salad for breakfast?"

His cheeks reddened slightly. "Is that not appropriate?"

"Who am I to say?" she answered lightly. "I've eaten

Oreos for dinner."

"Oreos?"

"Come, I'll let you try one while I make breakfast as I am unfortunately out of tuna."

Benjamin's face fell, and she motioned him to follow her to the kitchen. "I'll be right back," she excused herself, and dashed off to her bedroom. She was still embarrassed that he'd seen her in her pajamas. She pulled on a blue, full-length cotton bathrobe. Her cheeks burned as she remember his eyes travelling down her body.

My dear, Miss Bell, you are only providing me additional evidence to support my case, came Sherlock. *You have succumbed to the basest of human instinct.*

"Go away," she muttered as tying the belt of her robe.

She waited for him to speak again. Relieved when he didn't, she rejoined Benjamin in the kitchen.

"You ate the rest of the tuna last night. When I go out to see Flora, I'll stop by the grocery store and pick up some more." She tried not to smile as she glanced at her ill-fitting clothes. "I think I'll stop at the thrift store too, and see if I can find you some clothes that actually fit."

"You are extremely kind." He pulled at the shirt a little as she started a pot of coffee. "I must admit this garment is rather constricting."

She finished the coffee and pulled a box of Oreos from a cupboard, handing him one of the chocolate sandwich cookies. "Here."

He took it, turning it over a few times before taking a tentative bite. His eyes widened as chewed, and closed moments later, the rest of the cookie was in his mouth as he munched away in ecstasy. "Oh my," he moaned, his mouth still full of cookie.

She smiled and nodded as she threw a few slices of bacon in a pan.

He looked at her as he swallowed the last bite. "Better than tuna salad."

"Much better," she smiled.

He eyed the package of cookies longingly and Irene suppressed a laugh.

"Would you like another one?"

"If you could spare one," he reasoned, although he didn't hesitate to take the proffered treat.

He ate the second cookie a bit slower than the first, sniffing as the smell of frying bacon filled the air. "Mmm. Bacon. Is all the food in this day delicious?"

Irene laughed as she put the cooked bacon on a paper towel covered plate, drained the bacon grease into a can. "I promise you it is not. And unfortunately, those cookies are terribly bad for you," she gave him a pointed look as she caught him reaching for the Oreos.

He froze guiltily before sliding the package back on the table.

"Pretty much everything that tastes good is bad for you. It'll either make you fat or make you sick."

His face fell, but a moment later, a crafty grin crossed his face. "However, I will only be here a week regardless of what happens, so it is moot." He put a hand on the package and gave her a questioning glance.

Irene exploded with laughter. "Go for it. Have as many as you like."

Smiling with the joy of a child, he opened the cookies and pulled one, then two, and after a moment's hesitation, a third cookie from their slotted tray.

"You are a kind woman, Irene," he sighed as he bit a

cookie in half.

"Hey," she shrugged. "I understand the love of a good cookie."

He munched his cookies as he watched her cook. She cracked some eggs into the pan and minutes later, she slid them onto a plate along with a couple slices of bacon and handed it to Benjamin. "So, I've been thinking. If I have to go to the store and see Flora, I'm going to need someone to watch the store for me."

He paused mid-bite. "Surely you're not referring to me?"

She stared at him.

"I know nothing about your business. What if someone comes in and wishes to make a purchase?"

She shrugged. "After what I saw last night, I highly doubt anyone will come in today. It was chaos out there," she motioned in the direction of the town square.

He leaned toward her, his eyes lit with curiosity. "What exactly did you see?"

"I saw a man turn into a wolf and a woman sprout wings. I watched what looked like a vampire attack a woman." Remembering, she shuddered a little. "I hid after that until a light hit the store and I found you downstairs."

His mouth gaped a little. She held up a hand and nodded. "I know how crazy it sounds. The stuff of fiction, right? But I swear to you, most of the time I'm very prudent. I'm not prone to believe in fairy tales. I wouldn't have believed it if I hadn't seen it with my own eyes."

"Wolfmen and vampires," he shook his head.

"And ghosts," she cocked her head toward him.

"Point taken."

"Anyway, I need you to watch the store for me," she

continued. "I'll show you how to use the cash register. It isn't hard, and like I said, I doubt we'll get many customers today."

He sighed as he finished his last bite of food. "Very well. I will assist you."

"Thank you."

CHAPTER SEVEN

Forty-five minutes later, the kitchen cleaned from breakfast, Irene showered and dressed in jeans and a t-shirt. Benjamin's hair combed and pulled back, they stood behind the counter in the store.

"Then you just hit the red cash button," she told him and watched as he repeated all the steps she'd shown him in perfect order. "Perfect. You'll do fine."

"I shall do my best."

Irene picked up her black woven purse and walked to the front door, unlocking it as she paused with her hand on the doorknob. "If you get bored you can read anything you like. That is, if you like to read," she amended.

"Thank you," he came out from behind the register. "I will do so."

With one last glance around her beloved bookstore and a nod, Irene walked out the door and closed it firmly behind her.

She turned to look out on the town square. The grass

was a frightful mess, matted in some places, and torn up in others. A crater the size of a Volkswagen had been gouged out in front of the statue of Peter Saint. Several of the shops along the square had windows smashed in and appeared to have been looted at some point.

She turned and walked down the sidewalk to the end of the square and tried the door of Clara's Closet, the local handmade clothing store. The door opened, much to her relief.

She turned to find Clara behind the counter, gripping a shotgun in both hands. Clara, gray-haired and never afraid to speak her mind, had owned the store for years.

She's not afraid to shoot intruders either, Irene thought as she eyed the gun.

"Clara, it's just me," she said, holding her hands up in front of her. "Irene, from the bookstore."

"Irene?" the old woman squinted at her before stashing the gun under the counter. "What are you doing here, girlie? Haven't you seen what's been going on? Why on earth would you be out wandering about right now? It's dangerous out there."

Irene glanced out the front window, realizing Clara was probably right. She'd never considered that the creatures she'd seen the night before might still be out wandering around the town. Then Benjamin's face ran through her mind and she realized if she really wanted to help him, she had no choice.

"I have an unexpected guest," she told Clara. "Showed up last night."

Clara grunted. "Well, you're not the first one to come in here today telling me the same thing."

"I need some clothes. I'm thinking a men's large."

"Over here," Clara directed her to several racks. Irene rifled through them, marveling at the quality of the garments. She quickly picked out a couple cotton shirts, a jacket, and two pairs of loose slacks. She added socks and boxer shorts to her purchases and looked around for shoes. Frowning, she deliberated, wondering what size Benjamin wore before finally deciding against the shoes altogether.

Piling her purchases on the counter, she waited while Clara rang her up.

"Be careful out there, girlie," Clara warned her as she handed Irene her change. "There are all sorts of things out there."

"I'll do my best," Irene answered. "You be careful too."

Clara smiled and took the shotgun back out from under the counter and patted it a couple times. "Don't you worry, I know how to take care of myself."

Irene left and walked back down to the bookstore to deliver the clothes to Benjamin. After all, if anyone did come in the store, he'd want to be a little more presentable.

The bell on the door jangled, startling Benjamin, who sat on the stool behind the counter. He flushed, dropping a book on the floor.

Irene narrowed her eyes as she took in his guilty expression. "What are you doing?" she asked.

"Nothing," his cheeks flamed, even behind his beard.

Irene raised an eyebrow. "Liar. What were you reading?" She walked behind the counter and picked up the book he'd dropped.

Her mouth fell open as she took in the cover. A woman bent over backward, her clothes nearly falling off her lush body, as her raven locks trailed down her back and a musclebound blond Viking held her in his arms, his bare chest pressed against her heaving chest. "Sweet Savage Love," she read off the cover.

"Benjamin," she gave him a look of profound disappointment. "Really? A bodice ripper? I was only gone for like twenty minutes."

He blushed even deeper, the red climbing clear up into his hairline. "I was just looking," he sputtered. "I've never seen a book such as this, with such images," he pointed to the couple. "I was curious."

She shook her head. "This is utter trash."

"Then why do you sell it?"

It was Irene's turn to blush. "Because it's popular and I sell a lot of it," she muttered. Remembering why she'd come back, she shoved the bag at him. "Here, clothes. I hope they fit."

"Thank you," he took the bag. "Will you stay until I change?"

She nodded and he hurried upstairs.

Once gone, she glanced at the couple on the book again. *They look a little like me and Benjamin*, she thought. Curious, she opened the book and read a few lines.

He drew close, standing in front of her. Touching her face, her soft skin a caress on his calloused warrior hands. She placed a hand over his and turned her face to kiss his rough palm, weathered by the years of yielding a sword.

"You quicken me," he whispered. "Like nothing before."

Her flowery scent filled the room, intoxicating him. He knew only that if he did not kiss her now he might die with desire. He leaned toward her, gathering her in his

67

arms. Her mouth parted slightly and he groaned as his lips captured hers.

Irene put the book down, her entire body on fire as she imagined Benjamin holding her like that and kissing her like that.

"Fool," she muttered to herself. "As far as he's concerned, he just saw his fiancée yesterday."

A moment later, Benjamin came back downstairs wearing one of the shirts and a pair of slacks. "These fit nicely," he told her spreading his arms out to show her. "I am in your debt."

Irene nodded, still flushed from the passage in the book. He walked across the store, coming to a stop directly in front of her. Close. Almost too close.

His brow wrinkled as he looked at her. "Are you well? You appear feverish." When his hand came out and touched her shoulder she jumped.

"I'm fine." She nearly ran toward the door. "I better get going. No time to waste. I'll be back as soon as I can."

She almost slammed the front door as she escaped the bookstore and the heat of his body and intense gaze.

"Get a hold of yourself," she breathed. "He's just a man. One that will be gone in less than a week."

With that thought in mind, she began the trek to Flora's house, a couple miles from the town square on the outskirts of town.

By the time she reached Flora's home, Irene found herself

wishing she owned a car for the first time in years. Saint's Grove was a walking town, and she had always enjoyed getting a little exercise on the short walk to the grocery store or wherever she needed to go, but Flora's house was a much further walk than the Food Giant. Of course, there were downed trees and blocked roads along the way so she never would have made it all the way in a car.

It was a ramshackle, two story Victorian and a painted wooden sign hanging from an iron fixture in the ground that read "Flora's Palm & Tarot Card Readings" creaked as it rocked back and forth.

Irene climbed the weathered wooden porch steps and knocked on the door. Wind chimes hanging from the porched tinkled as she waited.

Finally the door opened. Flora stared up at her for a moment, then sighed and directed her to come in. "I knew I'd see you again."

"Yes, well, I have something I want you to look at," Irene told her.

The tiny blonde woman sat in a floral armchair and motioned for Irene to sit in a matching chair on the other side of a small end table.

"Well?" Flora asked impatiently. "I've had visitors all morning and I imagine you won't be the last. Let's get on with this."

Irene pulled the drawing out of her purse and handed it to Flora.

"The Star Anthame," Flora gasped and her eyes flew to Irene's. "The hilt, more specifically. I've been around a long time and it's hard to surprise me but you've managed to do so. Where did you get this?"

"My father gave it to me," Irene answered, hesitating

for a moment before plunging in. "In a dream."

Flora leaned toward her. "Tell me more," she encouraged.

Irene gulped. "You believe me?"

She nodded vigorously, her hair bouncing slightly. "I have been around a long time, young lady. I've seen a great many things and I know that life is much like an iceberg. That which we cannot see far surpasses that which we can."

"Well," Irene thought for a moment, wondering where to start. "My mother always told me my father ran off when I was a baby, but the night of the eclipse I fell asleep on my balcony and dreamt of him." She told Flora about the story he'd told Irene, about visiting Professor McGurty, the artifact, the drawing he had made so he could study it. When she mentioned the strange woman who'd appeared in the college parking lot, Flora nodded.

"Priscilla," she muttered, her face a grim mask.

"Who is that?"

"Priscilla is the witch I told you about last night. She lives forever, possessing one person after another across the centuries. If your father was involved with the recovery of the Star Anthame, even peripherally ..." she shook her head. "I remember all the gossip around town, how folks were talking about your father, saying he'd run off, left a wife and baby over in Norfolk, never even went back to his sister's for his clothes. Just disappeared."

Tears threatened and Irene swallowed hard. "Momma never complained. She never said much of anything at all. Sometimes I wondered if she was different before he left. If maybe she talked more, smiled more."

Flora tapped her knee with a slender finger. "I never

knew your mother, but I did know your father. He was a curious, intelligent man with an open mind and heart. I never did believe that he would willingly abandon his family, no matter what the hens in town said."

A single tear escaped the corner of Irene's eye, and she wiped it away. "That's nice to hear."

Flora pulled a tissue from a box on the end table and handed it to Irene without looking at her. "Now, now, let's move on. Finish telling me about your dream."

Irene told her about the second dream the previous night.

"When I woke, I found the drawing in bed with me. Benjamin and I knew I had to come talk to you about it, show it to you," she concluded.

"And this is the transcription here?" Flora asked, pointing to the words on the bottom of the page. "Only when the planets align and one pure heart takes another with the blade will the power of the Star Anthame be broken."

"Do you know what it means?"

Flora's lips pressed together in a grim line. "Yes, I think I do. It is a prophecy. A deadly one."

A sense of dread washed over Irene. "That doesn't sound good."

"The first part of the prophecy has come true," Flora told her. "The planets have aligned and the doorway is still open, so there is still time. It is the second part ..." she shook her head.

"What?" Irene asked, irritated by how shrill her voice sounded. She leaned across the small end table and gripped Flora's hand. "What is the second part?"

Flora gripped her hand back, surprisingly strong as

she captured Irene's gaze. "There is a way to break the power of the Star Anthame, to cancel out every curse brought about by it."

"Well, that's it then!" Irene declared eagerly. "If we can destroy its power, Benjamin can cross over, right?"

Flora shrugged. "That I cannot say. He is here now. If you break the curse he could stay here or cross over. He may even enter a kind of purgatory, existing on neither side. It depends on him, what he wants, and if he has anything tying him here to this place and the power of the curse. The only thing I know for certain," she fixed her sharp eyes on Irene, gripping her hand even tighter, "Is that someone will have to die."

"What?"

Flora nodded. "One pure heart takes another with the blade," she repeated. "It means an innocent will have to take another innocent with the blade. You, Irene."

Irene felt faint. "What do you mean, me?"

"You are an innocent. I can see it in your heart. You will have to make a sacrifice to save him." Flora leaned back, closing her eyes. She tsked a moment. Her body shuddered a bit when she spoke again and her voice seemed distant, almost foreign. "Sacrifice your innocence for his. Sacrifice him to save him."

As soon as Irene understood what the old woman was trying to tell her, she tried to rip herself away from the witch. Struggling to remove her hand from the old woman's grasp, she finally tore herself away. "No," she declared.

Flora seemed to come out of the trance she was in and her eyes were sad when she looked at Irene again.

"No!" Irene said with more force, her eyes wild.

"You're telling me I have to *kill* him?"

"Do you want to help him?"

"Of course," she gaped. "But you're asking me to do something I'm just not capable of."

"I'm not asking you to do anything," Flora shot back. "I'm simply telling you what you must do if you want to save him. What you actually do is entirely up to you."

"There has to be another way." Irene almost choked on the words, even as she knew the witch would provide her with no additional recourse.

Flora just stared at her and Irene decided it was time to leave. She stood and stared at the woman awkwardly. "Well. Thank you. I guess."

Sympathy washed over Flora's face and she stood, gathering Irene's hands in her own. "I'm sorry, child. It is obvious there is a connection between you and your ghost. You are struggling with the thought of losing him, aren't you?"

Irene blushed. "A connection? I'm not sure what you mean."

"Yes, you do."

Irene fell silent before nodding almost imperceptibly. "If I have any more questions, can I come see you again?"

"Of course," Flora answered, patting her on the shoulder as they walked to the door. "I will be here." She stood on the porch as Irene walked down the stairs and across the yard. "Irene," she called.

Irene turned back to look at her. "Yes?"

"I know you will go looking for another answer, but know this, the more time you spend looking for answers you won't find, the less time you'll have to look for the pieces of the Star Anthame. And there are others looking for it now too. You will have to find them and work to-gether." She gripped the edge of the door, her expression urgent. "Don't waste time looking for the impossible."

Irene nodded slowly. "I'll try to keep that in mind."

But as she walked down the path toward town again, there was only one thought on her mind.

How on earth am I going to tell Benjamin?

CHAPTER EIGHT

early two hours later, Irene finally made it back to the bookstore. It was midday and despite the clear skies and the brightly shining sun, the cool October weather gave her a bit of a chill. She was relieved when she walked through the door, not just for the heat but also for the chance to put down the grocery bags she'd carried several blocks.

She looked around the store for Benjamin as the front door closed behind her. Taking a few steps, she found him sitting at the table in the contemporary fiction room, engrossed in a book. Next to him on the table lay the package of Oreos from upstairs, now empty. "Benjamin?"

He jumped, flinging the book across the room, his face blazing.

Irene put a hand across her mouth, trying to smother her grin. She knew without looking he'd been reading another smutty book. Deciding to have a little fun with him, she walked across the room and leaned down to pick up the book.

"His Warrior Woman," she read out loud. She glanced at him, raising an eyebrow as she opened the book and read out loud.

"She slowly pulled the sheet down the length of his body, and he couldn't stop the slight shudder that ran through his body as she stood above him. Her skin bared for him, her delectable curves and creamy flesh a feast for his eyes. His gaze traveled lower and he caught a glimpse of her delectable jewel. His manhood stirred as his mouth went dry. He had imagined seeing her like this, but to have her so close now, ready, willing—it was almost more than he could bear.

She slithered up his body, pausing for a moment as her breasts met the junction of his thighs. He gritted his teeth as he fought the urge to grab her and turn her under him. He'd wanted her from the moment he laid eyes on her, and now, with her dark hair snaking around her body almost to her waist, dark eyes, and sweet, soft skin caressing his own, he nearly lost himself. He took in a ragged breath, desperate for control. His pleasure rod ... "

Irene nearly choked on the words and glanced back up at Benjamin. She found him studying the ceiling, bookshelves, table, looking everywhere but her, and she couldn't stop herself from laughing. His face was a brilliant scarlet, all the way to his ears.

"You know," she giggled, picking up the empty cookie package, "usually it's women laying around eating bonbons and reading sleazy romance novels."

"Romance," he sputtered, pointing a finger at the book. "I'd hardly call that romance."

"Neither would I," Irene agreed. "However, millions

of women across the world would disagree with us."

"I did not intend to eat all the cookies," he apologized.

She grinned and pointed across the room to the grocery bags she'd set on the floor next to the counter. "It just so happens I brought home another package. I'll let it go if you help me carry the bags upstairs."

"Of course, my lady," he nodded, hurrying to pick them up. "It would be my pleasure."

She locked the front door, hung a sign with an adjustable clock set at one o'clock on it, and followed him upstairs. After setting her purse on the kitchen table, she motioned for Benjamin to sit while she put the groceries away. "Did anyone come in today?" she asked.

"You had two guests, although remarkably, one was from my time."

"What!" She turned to stare at him. "From your time? You mean he was a ghost too?"

He shook his head. "No. From what I gathered, he moved through time. His name is Albert. And I'm afraid his companion took a book and did not pay for it." He frowned. "I let him leave with it because Albert told me he was helping him get back to his time and needed the book to do so."

"What book?"

Benjamin shook his head. "I am sorry, Irene. I tried to find out but a woman burst in, demanding they follow her. It seemed urgent, so I let them go. Are you upset?"

"No, of course not. Everything is a little crazy right now. If we're dealing with this," she waved a hand at him. "I can only imagine there are other people in town dealing with equally crazy situations."

"That does make sense," he nodded.

A time traveler," she breathed, sitting down in a chair as the impact of it all hit her. She shook her head in disbelief. "I saw some amazing things last night. I wonder what other myths, legends and science fiction stories have come to life."

Benjamin frowned as he fingered a plastic bag. "Intriguing, I agree. However, before I forget, I have been meaning to ask you about this material. What is it? I've never seen such stuff in my life."

"It's plastic," Irene answered. "It's made from petroleum, plant fibers sometimes."

His blank look had her waving him off. "We have more important things to talk about than plastic."

Flora's explanation of the prophecy ran through her mind and she jumped out of the chair and started making lunch as a means of distraction. "So, we have to look for the pieces of the Anthame."

"We already knew that."

"Yes," Irene agreed, "but what we didn't know before was that other people are looking for the pieces too."

"Did the witch tell you that?"

"Mm-hm." Irene dumped a can of tuna in a bowl and added mayonnaise, mustard and some seasoning, mixing it with a spoon. "She said we will have to work together. With the others, I mean."

Benjamin sniffed with interest. "Did she tell you who?"

Irene opened her mouth to answer, then frowned. "No, as a matter of fact. And I didn't ask. Why didn't I think to ask?"

You have been distracted, my dear Miss Bell. As I

previously stated. Holmes' sounded disappointed. *Now that you've succumbed to your base emotions, your ability to examine a situation with a clear, concise thought process has been compromised.*

"It has not," she replied hotly.

"What?"

Irene startled, turning to find Benjamin just inches from her. He looked down at her, and as her eyes traveled up his chest and to his face, she couldn't stop herself from thinking about the passage from the romance novel she'd read aloud.

For just a moment she let herself imagine the two of them in a similar situation. She let herself pretend she was bold and sensual with the ability to let go and frolic naked with a man, like the woman in the romance novel. She pictured Benjamin reacting like the warrior, his hard body hardening even more for her.

"Are you ill, Miss Bell?" he whispered, staring down at her with eyes that burned her skin. "You look feverish again."

She found her gaze focused on his lips and the way they moved as he talked. For a moment, a fraction of a second, her body leaned toward his so she could place her lips on his. She realized her mouth was mere inches from his and she drew in a sharp breath.

He seemed to be holding his. "You must think me a cad," he breathed. "It seems only yesterday I saw Stella, and yet, you are here." He closed the distance between them slightly, until she could feel his breath on her cheek. "You confuse me so."

She shivered. "Benjamin," she whispered. "Please."

She didn't know what she asked of him, even as the

word left her mouth. Was she asking him to back away? Kiss her?

Both, perhaps? Asked Holmes.

Yes, both. She wanted to kiss him and she didn't. Being so close to him was the most sensual experience of her life, and yet she could hardly bear it.

Her breath hitched as his face dipped, his lips so close to hers she could swear she felt them brush against each other.

What about Stella? Her mind screamed. *Stella. Stella, Stella, Stella, Stella!*

She took a step backward until she was pressed against the counter, desperate to get away from his intoxicating presence.

Benjamin took a step back as well, confusion muddling his expression. "Miss Bell, please let me express my sincerest apologies. I have no excuse for my behavior." His face darkened as the corners of his mouth dipped down. "I am finding it difficult."

"Difficult?" she gulped. "What do you mean?"

He moved away, taking with him the heat and intensity of his nearness, and Irene couldn't stop the little wave of regret that swept over her. "You are very winsome," he explained.

Winsome. She felt warm inside at the compliment. Everything about him seemed to make her warm on the inside.

What is wrong with me? She bit her lip and turned back to the lunch she'd been preparing.

I've told you already, came Holmes. *You are a slave to base biology. It is a natural state we must either overcome, or submit to. You know, of course, what I recom-*

mend.

I am not a slave to base biology, she responded hotly. *I have never been like this about any man. Which means there's something special about Benjamin. He's different.*

How so?

I don't know. She spooned tuna salad onto a piece of bread. *I just know this is not the same. I've been able to look at men objectively, acknowledge they are handsome, but never have I had to fight an attraction to one.*

Are you sure?

"Never," she declared, slapping a second piece of bread on the sandwich.

"What?"

She whirled to find Benjamin seated at the table again, his brow wrinkled as he looked up at her. Her cheeks flamed and she put the sandwich on a plate and handed it to him.

"Nothing," she lied. "Never mind."

His eyebrow lifted, announcing his disbelief, but he didn't push the matter. "I believe we were discussing the witch," he said as he took a large bite of his sandwich, moaning with satisfaction. "What else did she tell you? Did she understand the words on the knife?"

"The hilt," she corrected. "And yes, she had some thoughts."

She turned back to the counter, busying herself with cleaning crumbs and washing the few dishes.

"Are you going to share them?"

She turned and sat down across the table from him, her hands twisting in her lap as she studied the light floral pattern of the tablecloth and recalled Flora's words. When she finally spoke, it was with a strained voice. "She said it was a prophecy. That the power of the Star Anthame could be broken."

Benjamin rubbed his chin. "And that is bad?"

"No," she sighed. She looked up, beseeching him with her eyes. "She said someone has to die to break the curse. One innocent person has to kill another innocent person with the knife."

"Who?"

"She didn't say specifically. But …" She wrung her hands, almost ready to cry.

"But she had an idea," he finished grimly.

Irene nodded, a few tears finally slipping down her cheek. "She seemed to go into a trance and then she said 'sacrifice your innocence for his. Sacrifice him to save him.' She also told me I was an innocent. The implication being …" She wiped the tears away, unable to continue.

Benjamin nodded. "I see," he responded slowly. "You and I."

"Yes!" Irene leaned across the table, burying her face in her arms.

"And will that allow me to cross over?"

"I don't know," came Irene's muffled sobs. "She said maybe. Or that you might stay here. Or that you might be sent to some sort of purgatory. She didn't seem to have a damn clue!" she snapped.

"The only thing she seemed sure of was that we need to assemble the pieces of the Star Anthame, other people are looking for it, and I have to- to- *kill* you to break the power of the knife." She finally looked up at Benjamin, her face streaked with tears and crumpled with anguish. "How can I possibly do something so awful? I can't. I just can't."

Benjamin came around the table in a flash and knelt next to her chair, gathering her into his arms. "Shh," he soothed. "Do not cry. It pains me to see you so distraught."

She threw her arms around his neck and buried her head in his shoulder, letting her tears and frustrations and fears from the last twelve hours pour out onto his shirt.

He let her cry out her frustration for a few moments. When her sobs began to subside a little, he placed a gentle finger under her chin and lifted her face to meet his gaze. "Come now," he said with eyes full of concern. "There are many things outside of our control, this being no exception, but I am certain all will turn out as it should."

"How can you be so sure?" she asked brokenly.

"Because God makes no mistakes," he smiled. "All that is happening right now, all that *has* happened, it was part of a bigger plan. We are exactly where we are meant to be."

As Irene felt herself falling into the depths of his eyes, she wondered if that meant she was supposed to be wrapped up in his arms.

I hope so, she thought suddenly, blushing at her own brazen thought even while her tears still flowed.

Benjamin studied her, his brow furrowing. His arms tightened around her, the warmth of him seeping into her body. She drew in a breath and he frowned a little. "Irene, I do not pretend to understand all that has happened, yet I do understand that something is happening here, with you."

Irene flushed for what seemed like the millionth time since she found Benjamin in her store. "Yes," she whispered.

"It makes no sense."

"No," she agreed.

"We only just met."

She nodded.

"And for me it seems that I saw Stella only yester-day."

The corners of her mouth tipped down. "I know."

"And yet," his arms tightened around her. "Somehow, it seems so very long ago. Or even like a dream, something I imagined but was never actually so."

"A dream?" she echoed, wiping away the last of her tears.

It was his turn to nod. "So long ago," he murmured, almost to himself. "And only this, being here with you seems real."

She watched his gaze drop to her lips. She'd been pretty sure before, but for the first time she knew without a doubt he wanted to kiss her. The thought thrilled her, deep inside to the pit of her belly, and before she realized she'd done so, her lips parted in invitation.

"Irene," he whispered, and closed the distance be-tween them.

Soft lips brushed against hers once, twice, and she sighed.

Benjamin groaned at the sound, and the kiss turned from gentle to stormy. His mouth slanted across hers, nip-ping, teasing, caressing until Irene felt like her entire body was on fire.

His tongue traced the line of her bottom lip before plunging in to taste her. Irene whimpered with delight.

She let her tongue dance with his as his scent, woody and manly, filled her senses. His mouth moved across her cheek and down her neck.

Irene had never felt such pleasure. Every nerve ending in her body seemed to be at attention, and as he plundered the soft spot behind her ear, she gave into the sensation and let her head fall back, reveling in the moment.

Benjamin pulled her off her chair onto his lap and she willingly wrapped herself around him, her soft, lush curves pressing against the hard planes of his body.

A moment later, she found herself laying on the floor, the cold linoleum tiles pressed against her back and his hot, hard body pressed against her front.

His hands reached for hers and he pulled her arms above her head as his mouth covered hers again. She writhed underneath him and he groaned against her mouth. His hips moved against hers, gyrating ever so lightly but enough that Irene could feel his arousal.

"Benjamin," she gasped, struggling to pull her hands from his grip so she could wrap her arms around him.

He froze. A moment later he was across the room and Irene lay alone on the cold floor, missing the warmth of him, panting, confused, and terribly embarrassed as she realized she'd completely lost control.

She struggled to her feet, too mortified to meet his gaze. Tears pricked at her eyes again as she wondered what he was thinking. *Women from his time didn't act like that,* she thought with horror. *Only whores and ... and slatterns.*

"No, Irene," Benjamin said gently, seemingly reading her mind. "Do not think such things. The fault is mine. I took advantage of you."

She barked a laugh and much to her dismay, her tears began flowing again. She turned her back to him. Irene couldn't remember the last time she cried, and here she was, crying for the third time in one day. "I practically threw myself at you. I promise I don't usually behave like that. I'm usually much more reserved. I don't know what's gotten into me."

"I behaved like a complete cad," he apologized. "I assure you, it will not happen again."

Somehow his assurance made her feel worse.

"Fine, good," she mumbled. "We need to focus on finding the pieces of the knife anyway."

"Irene."

She dashed away her tears with one hand before taking a deep breath and turning to look at him.

His eyes shimmered with concern. "Despite the memory of Stella and despite my shame, I have wanted to kiss you from the moment I first opened my eyes and saw you standing above me. Yes, I fought it, but it was there, even when I believed you to be a witch. I cannot explain it, this thing between us." He gripped the edge of the table. "Tell me I am wrong. Tell me you do not feel it as well."

She sat down across from him. "I think you know better than that. I can't explain it either."

"Yes," he nodded. "And now, knowing that I will be gone in mere days, no matter how much I want to … how can I-? How can we-?"

He didn't need to finish either sentence for Irene to understand his meaning.

A very sensible caution, came Holmes voice. *He is a prudent man, much like myself. Of course, I would never have let myself kiss you in the first place.*

You never would have wanted to in the first place, she shot back.

True. I have never been susceptible to the charms of a

86

woman, not even one with charms as obvious as yours.

Irene felt her temper flare. "Boorish man," she muttered.

"What?"

"I said it would be foolish," she lied. "And you are right. We should be concentrating on finding the pieces of the knife, not this, whatever," she waved a hand back and forth between them.

He seemed slightly relieved, although a shadow of a frown still seemed to darken his face. "Yes, he responded. "But I haven't the slightest clue where to start."

"I have one idea. It may not pay off, but it's all I have right now."

"What are you thinking?"

She reached for her purse, still on the table, and pulled out the drawing. She laid it out so they both could see it. "You need to understand a few things first."

She told him briefly about her childhood, about her father's disappearance, then his story about visiting his sister and Professor McGurty.

"Flora knows all about the Star Athame, but the professor actually had the hilt at some point. He may still have it. And he may know something about the other pieces. At this point, it's the only lead I have. He's the only person in town besides Flora that we know for sure has any knowledge of it. He may know something she doesn't." She tapped the drawing. "I think it's time to pay the good professor a visit."

CHAPTER NINE

A short time later, Irene found herself walking through the town square toward Saint's Grove Community College.

She had no idea if Professor McGurty was in his office or if classes were still being held today. Several of the shops in the square had broken windows and bore evidence of looting. Only a handful were actually open, and the entire square was missing the usual midday bustle of activity.

When she reached the college, she knew classes had been canceled for the day due to the nearly empty parking lot. However, Professor McGurty's rusty little red Toyota pickup sat in one corner, so she headed for his office.

After navigating the hallways of the school, she stood in front of his office, the door closed. She knocked and heard his muffled voice a moment later.

"Who is it?"

"Professor," she called gently. "It's Irene Bell. I need

to talk to you."

"How do I know it's really you?"

She tried the door but found it locked.

"You can't come in!" he called sharply. "Like I said, how do I know it's really you?

What a strange question, she thought until the story of the witch possessing people through the years ran through her mind. *Maybe not so strange after all. Not to mention if he suspects I'm not who I say I am, he knows something about what's going on.*

"Professor, I really need to talk to you. I have something to show you. My-" she took a deep breath and decided to plunge in and tell him the truth. "My father gave it to me. I know you were the last person to see him before he disappeared. He told me about the artifact."

No response came, but a moment later she heard the door unlock. He cracked the door open enough to poke his head through. It was almost comical, his gray hair wild as he looked through his square glasses perched at the end of his long, crooked nose. He peered up and down the hall before stepping back and opening the door just wide enough to let Irene in. Once she stood next to him, he immediately closed the door and locked it once more.

A thin, older man, often buzzing with the nervous energy of a hummingbird, he seemed even more agitated than usual. Patting her on the shoulder, he held out a hand toward the saggy brown couch along one wall. "Sit, sit."

I did, trying to find a comfortable position on the flat cushions as the professor sat in his desk chair and turned to face me, his eyes accusatory. "I never told a soul that your father was here the night of his disappearance. Nor have I spoken of the artifact since that day. How is it you know about it?"

I pulled the drawing out of my purse. "My father gave me this," I answered as I handed it to him.

He took the piece of paper and glanced at it. His gaze widened and he pushed his glasses up to get a better look before fixing me with sharp eyes. "Where did you get this?"

"I told you, my father gave it to me."

"Impossible," he scoffed. "I watched him draw it the night he disappeared. He had it on his person."

"Yes," I agreed. "And I know how crazy this is going to sound, but you know me to be a fairly logical person." She tucked a stray lock of hair behind her ear with shaking fingers. "My father has appeared to me in what I thought was a dream but now know to be something more. Twice now. Yesterday before the meteor hit near the statue of Peter Saint, and I just dismissed it as a strange dream. But then he appeared again last night. He gave me that drawing and had me write the translation down." I pointed to the paper in his hand. "When I woke, it lay on the bed next to me."

Professor McGurty's mouth fell open and he looked at the drawing with new interest. "Fascinating," he breathed.

I pushed on. "He told me that a woman approached him as he left your office all those years ago, and afterward he found himself somewhere else, as he put it. Here but not here. And after some of the things I've seen and learned about the world since last night, I'm guessing he's in a sort of limbo."

His expression piqued with interest. "What have you seen?"

She shuddered a little. "Were you in the square last night?"

He shook his head. "No, I worked late last night grading papers. I finished not long after dark and got in my car to drive home, and …" he trailed off as he remembered. "One strange thing after another. It is as if every myth and legend about Saint's Grove has been coming to life."

She leaned forward eagerly. "Yes," she breathed. "I saw a man change into a wolf right in front of my eyes last night. And a woman grew wings and flew off into the sky. And, and a *vampire killed a woman.*"

He shook his head with bemusement. "Something that looked like a giant wolf jumped in front of my truck on the way home."

"Another werewolf," Irene exclaimed.

"It would seem," he agreed. "And earlier today, Lisa from the museum came knocking on my door." His eyes grew fearful. "I've worked with her and her brother Mark before, identifying and dating certain artifacts, so naturally I trusted her. But when I let her in, she seemed … very unlike herself. She kept asking me about a hilt. I had no idea what she was talking about, but the more I denied any knowledge, the angrier she became. I finally pointed out her strange behavior and tried to make a joke to cut the tension."

"What did you say?"

He gave her a wry grin. "I said 'who are you and what have you done with Lisa?' Her response, was …" he shuddered a little. "A terrible expression crossed her face and she told me Lisa was safe for the time being, but if I wanted her to stay that way, I better give her the hilt. I told her again that I didn't know what she was talking about and asked her to leave. She did, yelling at me the whole time and told me she'd be back tonight and I better have the hilt."

Irene's eyes widened. "Very strange."

"Indeed. That's when I realized the possibility that people in town could be someone other than who they claimed to be. And that's why I was so fearful when you knocked on my door, and why I asked how I could know you were you." He put his hands on his knees, leaning toward her. "Honestly, I don't know what to do. I don't know anything about a hilt."

"I think I can answer that question." She reached out to him, gripping his hand in hers. "A man appeared in my store. A man who's been dead for almost a hundred and fifty years. A ghost."

His eyes lit up. "Truly? A ghost?" he smiled a little and leaned toward her even more. "Can you touch him? See through him? How do you know he's a ghost?"

Irene smiled at despite the seriousness of the situation. "He looks like a man, is flesh and blood like a man as long as he stays in the bookstore. It used to be his office," she explained. "Do you know the old woman Flora who lives on the outskirts of town? The palm reader?"

He nodded and she continued. "We had an interesting encounter with her last night, and I visited her again this morning. She says he's cursed, bound to the place he was murdered. The drawing my father gave me, the artifact is just one piece of a knife called the Star Anthame, a powerful weapon created by witches. When an evil witch took control of it and used it for her own purposes, her coven stole it back, broke it up, and hid the pieces. The evil witch still lives by possessing people, jumping from body to body. She's been searching for the pieces ever since. According to Flora, if I can get the three pieces of the knife, we can break the curse put on Benjamin and he can cross over." She frowned at the thought.

The professor patted her knee. "You don't seem very happy about that fact."

She waved him off. "That doesn't matter. We have no choice in the matter. But that's why I'm here." She pointed to the drawing. "You were the last person to see this piece. This is the hilt."

His eyes lit up. "Ah! A piece of the puzzle revealed! But what does Lisa want with it?"

Irene shook her head. "I don't know, but it might be possible that the evil witch has possessed her. In which case, I'm not sure what we can do. And I promised I would help Benjamin. According to Flora, we only have a week before the rift between worlds closes. If we can't break the curse before then so he can cross over, he'll be trapped in limbo for a thousand years."

"What about Lisa? We have to try and help her too."

She shook her head with frustration. "I don't have the time to run all over Saint's Grove trying to help the entire town. And I have to think that Mark knows something is going on with his sister and will do what he can to help her."

He studied Irene for a moment. "Benjamin is the ghost?"

"Yes." She squeezed his hand, trying to convey the urgency she felt. "Flora also told me that I'm not the only one looking for the pieces. I don't know how many people in town besides myself and the witch are searching for it, but I'm determined to find it and help Benjamin."

"Why?" he asked curiously, even though he seemed to already know the answer. "I know you've always avoided too much involvement with folks around town, that you prefer your own company to that of others. Why do you care so much about helping this Benjamin fellow?"

She looked away. "He's stuck in my home. I want him out."

"But it sounds like either way he'll be gone in a week." He shrugged. "You could just hole up in your apartment and wait it out. Instead, you're out and about, putting yourself at risk amidst the craziness going on in town."

"I- I-" Her mouth opened and closed as she tried to come up with an appropriate response.

He smiled at her. "Think about it."

She felt her face flush and she nodded before pressing on. "Do you still have the hilt, Professor?"

His face fell, and she knew the answer before he said it. Looking down at their hands, he shook his head. "No. The night your father disappeared I said goodbye to him in the parking lot and drove home. When I arrived back at my office in the morning, I found it had been broken into and the artifact was gone."

Irene's heart sank and she let go of his hand. "Damn. It must have been the witch."

"I don't think so," Professor McGurty shook his head. "If Lisa has been possessed by the evil witch, we have to presume it was the same witch who cursed your father."

"That seems reasonable."

"Well, then, if she stole the artifact from me all those years ago, why wouldn't she remember doing so? Why did she come to me looking for it?" He let go of her hand and leaned back in his chair, rubbing his chin thoughtfully.

Irene gaped at him. "You're right."

"Unless …" he mused.

"Unless what?"

He shrugged a little. "If other people are looking for it, perhaps someone stole it from her. She came to me because she stole it from my office all those years ago and she was grasping at straws. I was the last person in possession of it before her. Maybe she thinks I stole it back again."

"Perhaps," Irene mused. "What do you know about it? Where did you find it?"

"I know very little about it, but I found it in the woods on the outskirts of town. There's an area deep in the forest that is considered one of the first homesteads in the area. There are several buildings still left and a number of artifacts have been found there." He waved a hand. "Of course, everything found there is considered to be relevant only to local historians, but it is still fascinating. The piece in question, however, I found hidden behind a loose hearthstone in one of the homes. It is thought that a lone woman lived there, very unusual for the time. Her name was Priscilla Meriwether."

"Priscilla," she gasped.

He leaned toward her. "The name is familiar to you?"

She nodded. "According to Flora, Priscilla is the evil witch."

He whistled long and low. "Do you believe in coincidence, child?"

"I, well, I guess I used to," she struggled to answer. "But now, the more I learn about what's going on in Saint's Grove, the more I doubt everything I've ever believed in."

"Agreed," he nodded. "Which leads me to believe we need to take a little hike."

"Where?'

"Why, to the old homestead, of course."

Two hours later, Irene found herself wishing she'd worn hiking boots. Her feet ached and she was pretty sure she had blisters on two of the toes on her left foot.

"Ah," declared Professor McGurty. "Here we are."

The trees widened into a little clearing, revealing the old homestead. A dozen or so buildings, most falling to the ground with their wooden planks rotted and dank, littered the edge of the clearing.

The professor led her to one of the better preserved houses. "This is where I found the hilt." He carefully opened the door and led Irene inside.

After her eyes adjusted from the lack of light, she looked around. Any furniture that had been in the home had long since been removed. Sparse weeds and grass grew up from the dirt floor, weak and sickly looking from the lack of sun.

"Here," the professor led her to the hearth and tapped a stone. "This one is loose and has a secret compartment behind it." He frowned. "It looks as though it has been freshly disturbed."

Irene reached out a trembling hand and pulled on the stone. After a moment's resistance, it came out easily and

Irene handed it to Professor McGurty. "If the witch used this as a hiding place before, why would she use it now? It's already been discovered, why run the risk of using it again."

He lifted an eyebrow. "Human nature, child. We are creatures of habit, even the craftiest, most clever of us."

Irene reached into the crevasse. "I think there's something in there," she breathed.

"Be careful," the professor warned.

A warning she should have heeded as she pricked her finger on something sharp. "Ouch!"

She pulled her hand back to find a small cut on her forefinger. She sucked on it for a moment as the professor put the stone down and pulled a handkerchief out of his pocket and offered it to her. "Is it bleeding badly?"

She looked at her finger. "No, it's already slowing down." She glanced at the handkerchief. "However, I think I can still use that."

She took it and wrapped it around her hand before reaching back into the hole in the hearth, albeit this time with a little more caution. When she reached the object inside, she made sure to grasp it with the handkerchief.

"It's a blade," Professor McGurty exclaimed when she pull it out.

Excitement built up inside her. Indeed, it most certainly looked like a blade, and even though she'd never seen it, she was certain it belonged to the Star Anthame. It would be too much of a coincidence to be anything else.

She carefully wrapped the blade in the professor's handkerchief and put it in her purse. "I promise I'll wash it and return it."

He waved her off. "Keep it, my dear." Glancing

around the cabin, his brow wrinkled. "I think we should leave. If I am correct, and the stone has been moved recently, then the witch has been here and may be back any time. I definitely do not want to be here when she arrives."

Irene agreed and they put the stone back before leaving the cabin, making sure to close the door behind them.

The hike back to town seemed shorter and Irene felt light as a feather despite her throbbing feet, as she imagined going home and presenting Benjamin with the blade. She pictured the smile on his face and a little seed of warmth spread through her belly. She'd never seen such a handsome man, nor one who made her feel so-

You should focus on your task at hand, my dear Miss Bell, came Holmes. *Fanciful thoughts of him will only hurt you in the end. Do not forget what you must do. Do not forget when this is over, he will be gone forever.*

This time, Irene ignored her idol, refusing to respond. The ache that arose in her chest at his words, however, was impossible to ignore, and suddenly her throbbing feet felt heavy as bricks.

She knew Holmes spoke the truth. No matter what happened, whether she succeeded or failed, Benjamin would be gone by the end of the week.

You only just met him, she admonished herself. *Despite the kiss earlier, he's a complete stranger. Why does it matter to you if he stays or goes?*

Yet somehow, she knew it did matter to her. It mattered very much.

CHAPTER TEN

By the time Irene and Professor McGurty made their way back to town, the sun had begun to set. Glancing at the old man beside her, she wondered when he'd gotten so thin. The day had exhausted him as well, and Irene found herself worrying over him.

"Professor, please come over to the house and have dinner. It won't be fancy, but you look so tired and you've been such a big help today." Irene couldn't help but wonder what had gotten into her. She never invited people over for supper.

Professor McGurty, however, perked up at the offer. "That's very kind of you, my dear. I must admit, I have a strong desire to meet this ghost of yours. Will he be there as well?"

She nodded. "He can't leave the store. When he tried, his body began to disappear."

"Fascinating," he exclaimed. "I must say this about what happened yesterday, we are having experiences we'll remember for the rest of our lives."

"If we can manage to come out of it alive," she quipped, all too aware of the irony.

He chuckled. "Yes, there is great risk, isn't there?" He shook a finger at her. "But the rewards are great too. All things worth having are like that. The best things in life are the things we suffer the most for."

"Perhaps," Irene murmured. He stopped walking, and she glanced at him. "What?"

"You know what your problem is, Irene?"

She flushed. "I didn't realize I had a problem."

He continued as if she hadn't spoken at all. "Your problem is that you've never wanted anything enough to risk putting yourself out there. I mean, sure, you love your store, your books, but is that really enough? Are you truly satisfied? No," he held up a hand. "Don't answer that. I'm not sure if you are truly aware of how unhappy and lonely you've been."

Irene gaped at him. "What's gotten into you, Professor?"

"I care about you," he shot back. "Your father was a dear friend and the best student I ever had. I've watched you hide inside your shell for years, ever since you came to live with your Aunt Caroline. I've waited to see you start really living, but you never have. You've hidden in your books.

"But now, for the first time ever, I'm watching you put yourself out there. You're connecting with someone. A real person, not a character from one of your books." The professor paused a moment. "Even if he is a ghost."

Irene felt her face burn with embarrassment as the image of Holmes flashed through her mind. He was right.

She spent more time talking to a character inside her mind than any real person.

When had it happened? Why had she never realized how far she'd sunk?

They reached the edge of the town square, and she stood for a moment, studying her little bookstore at the opposite end. The lights in the store were all shut off while a soft glow emanated from upstairs. She wondered what Benjamin was doing.

Probably reading another sleazy romance. She smiled at the thought and glanced back at the professor. "You're right," she confessed softly.

His eyebrows shot up. "Well, that was surprisingly easy. I hardly expected you to agree with me."

She glanced at the grass beneath her feet. "It's not like I'm thrilled you pointed it out, but I'd be lying if I said I haven't spent more time alone with my books than with other people. But we can talk about that another time." She pointed toward her house. "Right now, my priority is Benjamin. As long as I'm putting myself out there for someone else, I'd like to do it right."

"Very well, my dear girl." He stepped closer to her and put an arm around her. "For what it's worth, I think you're a delightful young lady. Your father would have been proud."

She blushed at his praise. "That's good to hear."

"It must be remarkable to be able to talk to him." He pushed his glasses up, giving his head a little shake. "Such a remarkable opportunity to observe all the fascinating events unfolding, to take part in the mysteries that touch different planes of existence."

"Are you scared?" Irene looked at him with astonishment.

He clapped his hands together and rubbed them with vigor. "Oh yes, terrified. But still, this is more than just front row seats to a remarkable show. We are not just an audience, we are part of the cast. Werewolves, vampires, winged creatures, ghosts, witches, and who knows what else. All the myths and legends one can think of coming to life. It's an anthropologist's dream. Gods coming to life."

She laughed a little at his enthusiasm as she climbed the steps to the front door of the bookstore. "Well, why don't you come meet another myth," she smiled at him as she unlocked the door.

She led him through the store and upstairs.

Irene's small living room sat just off the landing at the top of the stairs, and she saw Benjamin sitting on the couch reading a book, his back to them.

"Benjamin," she said softly.

He jumped, flinging the book away from himself, before standing to greet them with blazing cheeks.

Irene stifled a laugh as the professor stepped forward. "My goodness, we surely didn't mean to scare you!" He walked around the couch to retrieve Benjamin's book. "You must have been quite engrossed in your work. That is, I mean to say, it must have been quite fascinating …" he trailed off as he glanced at the cover.

Benjamin's face burned bright red and after glancing at him, the professor began to chuckle a little. "No need for embarrassment, dear boy. I've been known to pick up a bodice ripper a time or two during my lifetime." He winked at the younger man.

Benjamin gaped at him for a moment. "Who are you?"

Irene stepped forward. "I'm so sorry, I seem to have forgotten my manners. Benjamin Churchill, I'm pleased to introduce you to Professor McGurty."

The professor grasped Benjamin's hand in his, shaking it with vigor. "So very pleased to meet you, young man." He laughed. "Well, not so young, really, are you? But then again, you don't look much like a ghost. Nothing spooky or scary about you, is there?"

Benjamin stared at the older man for a moment before a small smile crossed his face. "No, I suppose I don't much resemble a ghost. But then, I've never met one, so I really have no idea what one is supposed to look like."

Professor McGurty laughed again, clapping Benjamin on the shoulder. "Truer words, my boy!"

Benjamin glanced at Irene, then back at the Professor. "I'm assuming by your words and your presence Irene has shared my predicament with you?"

"He knows," she nodded, motioning for them to follow her to the small kitchen. "I hope you don't mind keeping me company while I make supper."

"Not at all," the professor replied with a cheery smile. "As long as you let me help you."

"I'd be happy for the help."

Bejamin smirked a little. "A chef and a professor?" he quipped.

"Indeed," he answered. "You'll find things are much different in this day and age. Men spend as much time in the kitchen as women. We've gone through women's rights, civil rights, the 60's, sex, drugs, and rock and roll."

"Sex, drugs, and rock and roll?" Benjamin parroted with a wrinkled brow.

The professor grinned. "Oh yes. Marriage is no longer

a prerequisite to sex for men *or* women, people take certain drugs for fun, and rock and roll is the music of a new generation."

Benjamin looked dazed at this new influx of information.

Professor McGurty laughed lightly and steered the conversation in another direction. "We can talk about all that later. Irene tells me you hail from almost one hundred and fifty years ago. Things here must seem very strange. A most fascinating situation to find yourself in, I might add."

Benjamin frowned. "Perhaps, yet I am trapped in this house while Irene puts herself in danger for me. I find it nearly intolerable."

"Benjamin." Irene's mouth fell open. "I had no idea you felt that way."

"How could I not?" he frowned. "It pains me to think of you, such a tender woman, risking yourself for me."

Irene fought a wave of annoyance at his words, and briefly thought of throwing the package of chicken she'd just pulled out of the fridge at his head. Instead, she turned and fixed him with an arch look. "That's why I enlisted the help of the good professor. I couldn't be expected to do this on my own, after all."

Professor McGurty burst out laughing at the expression of shocked dismay that crossed Benjamin's face. "Young man," he chortled. "I can assure you, Irene is a shockingly intelligent and capable woman. And one who clearly does not appreciate having her abilities called into question."

Benjamin's dismay still evident, he crossed the room to put a strong hand on Irene's shoulder. "I meant no disrespect, I just worry for you." He frowned. "And I am wholly frustrated by my inability to do a single thing to help you."

Irene felt herself soften a little at his words, but still felt the need to emphasize her point. "I have been on my own for many years, Benjamin." She lifted her chin. "I can take care of myself."

He reached up and pushed her hair behind an ear. "I meant no insult, nor do I think you incapable." He turned away. "However, you cannot know how confining it is to be stuck in this house, my fate left in the hands of another. It's maddening to have so little control. It's maddening to know you are out there for me and I must not only sit idly by, but I do not even know if you are safe."

Irene reached out and touched his shoulder. "I hadn't considered your point of view. I can see how hard it would be to feel so ..."

"Helpless?" the professor offered, and both Irene and Benjamin startled.

Irene flushed a little, realizing she had temporarily forgotten the older man was in the room.

"Yes," Benjamin nodded. "I can't recall ever feeling so helpless in my life."

Professor McGurty turned to Irene. "My dear, I believe we forgot to share our discovery with your young man."

She flushed at his words, but said nothing about it. "You're right," she nodded and retrieved the handkerchief wrapped blade from her bag and handed it to Benjamin. "How could I have been so thoughtless?"

Benjamin unwrapped the handkerchief, gasping slightly when he saw its contents. He set it down carefully on the table. "The blade." His eyes lit with excitement as he looked from Irene to the professor. "Where did you find it? Do you have the hilt as well?"

Professor McGurty's face fell. "I'm so sorry, but the hilt was stolen from me many years ago. I found it in the ruins of one of the original homesteads and had a hunch we might be lucky enough to find it there again. We didn't," he said regretfully before brightening. "However, we did find the blade."

Irene sat next to him. "I know it's frustrating to be stuck here, but I promise you, Benjamin, I'll do everything I can to help you."

The professor stood between them, a hand on each of their shoulders. "We both will," he announced. "But enough of this. We have much to discuss. We must decide what our next step will be, not to mention I'm famished."

Irene smiled. "We'd better finish dinner then."

They debated their next course of action over a supper of mushroom chicken and rice, green salad, two bottles of wine, and much laughter.

"We need to find the remaining pieces of the knife," Benjamin argued.

"Of course we do," Irene agreed, "but what if we break the curse and you still don't cross over? We need to find out why the witch cursed you in the first place. If you can take care of your unfinished business, you can cross over." She didn't mention that she was still terribly uncertain if she could fulfill the prophecy. The mere thought of hurting Benjamin with the knife, let alone stabbing him with it caused a great ache in her gut and a trembling panic.

"It has to be the Hawkins case," Benjamin told them. "I've had no involvement with anything else of any import, additionally, everything about the case was odd."

"We need to find out what happened to the farm" the professor decided. "And who was involved. We need to know who was behind SP Enterprises and if they still exist. What happened to Hawkins, Stone and anyone else involved. Sounds like we need to visit the courthouse."

"I agree," Irene nodded.

After much discussion, they'd settled on heading out in the morning to the courthouse, then the library if needed, assuming they didn't find what they were looking for in the town's public records.

"And please look into the fate of my brother Armin if you have time," Benjamin added. "He was a good man, but not very capable. I'd like to know what happened to him."

They decided after the courthouse visit, they'd meet back up with Benjamin and having a short lunch break. Afterward, if no other course of action presented itself, Irene and the professor would seek out Flora again and find out who else in town was looking for the Star Anthame. Perhaps they could all be more successful if they worked together, not to mention each might have information the other needed.

After all, they had the blade. Who knew what the others might possess.

Both Irene and Benjamin insisted the professor stay for the night, and at first Irene tried to give him her bed-

room. Horrified, Professor McGurty refused. "I could never put you out like that. It would be most ungentlemanly."
he objected, placing a hand over his heart dramatically. A
product of the wine, Irene assumed with a tiny smile.

He didn't argue too much with Benjamin, however,
when the younger man insisted on giving up the spare
room. "I will sleep right here," he patted the couch gaily,
also affected by the wine. "It will be a perfectly fine place
to sleep."

The professor tried to stifle a yawn before looking at
the two of them with regret. "Very well then. I'll take my
old bones to bed and leave you two be. It's way past my
bedtime."

Irene watched him trot off to the guest room, shaking
her head. "I hope when I'm his age I have as much energy."

Benjamin smiled. "Agreed. I like him very much."

"I do too."

They looked at each other, silence filling the space
between them. Irene stood awkwardly. "Well, I'm off to
bed too. We have a busy day tomorrow."

His eyes rested on hers for a moment. "Sleep well,
Irene," he murmured.

"You too." She found she couldn't tear her gaze away
from his. The memory of their kiss earlier in the day ran
through her mind, and she felt a rush of heat to her face as
well as in the pit of her belly.

"Irene," he whispered.

"Yes," she replied breathlessly.

"I-" A moment later he squeezed his eyes shut and
turned away from her. "You need your sleep. You should
go to bed, Irene."

Tears pricked her eyes and she nodded wordlessly before she fled the room.

She changed quickly and burrowed under her blankets before letting her tears fall.

You care for him, Holmes commented.

Yes. As much as I try to deny it, I do. What will I do?

You must disconnect yourself before you completely lose your objectivity. Already you look for excuses to ignore what you know to be true, to avoid what you must do.

What do you mean?

Playing coy, Miss Bell? Holmes sounded disappointed. *No matter what you tell yourself, you know you will have to break the power of the Star Anthame. It is the only way to prevent this sort of thing from happening again. The witch has already told you what you must do. Now, you must accept it.*

She sighed. "I know. What I don't know is how I'm supposed to do that."

Holmes didn't reply, and more tears streamed down her cheeks. Thoughts of other worlds, creatures and fate ran through her mind until finally she began to drift off to sleep out of pure exhaustion.

Still, her last thought was of Benjamin.

What kind of cruel fate would finally send me a man to love, only to take him away a week later?

CHAPTER ELEVEN

Day Three

"*I*rene." Her name sounded like a caress, sliding over her body and giving her chills.

She opened her eyes to find Benjamin above, his hair falling across his face and eyes warm, the color of melted chocolate as he gazed down at her.

"Benjamin," she sighed, reaching up and pushed his hair out of his eyes.

His smile seemed to hold a secret, one that existed only for the two of them. "Sweet girl," he breathed, just before he gathered her in his arms and his mouth swooped down to capture hers.

His soft lips danced across hers, teasing and plucking as his tongue dipped into her mouth to tangle with hers in *perfect harmony.*

She moaned and his hand moved up the length of her body until he cupped her cheek.

"I am enraptured by you," he whispered against her lips. "I cannot stop thinking about you."

"Oh, Benji," she shuddered. "I feel the same way."

She felt his mouth against hers as it spread into a grin. "Benji," he repeated. "No one has ever called me that."

"I won't if you don't like it."

"No, he shook his head ever so slightly. "Coming from your delectable lips, it is the sweetest endearment."

"Benji," she sighed again.

It was his turn to shudder. "Yes," he groaned just before his mouth took hers again.

The most intense desire Irene had ever felt exploded inside her, and she wrapped herself around him, pouring all her desire into the kiss.

As she wrapped her legs around his waist, one of his strong hands reached down and grasped her thigh. He pressed the length of his hard body against her soft one.

His mouth traveled across her cheek, then left a trail down her neck. I want you, Irene," he muttered fiercely, his hips gyrating against hers.

She groaned her response. "Yes."

"Irene."

She pressed herself against him. "Yes."

"Irene." His body disappeared from hers and she whimpered in protest.

"Yes," she murmured. "Come back."

"*Irene.*" His voice pressed.

"Why did you stop?" She stretched languorously. "Please, Benji. I want you too."

"Benji!" she heard laughter in his voice.

The tone of his voice finally broke through her haze and she opened her eyes to find Benjamin above her like her dream, except this time he neither held her nor had the same dreamy expression on his face.

No, this time his eyes danced with a combination of mischief and longing. After a moment's hesitation, he seemed to settle on mischief and he waggled his eyebrows. "Irene, perchance were you dreaming of me?"

Heat flooded her face and she dove under the covers. "No, of course not," she lied.

"You did," he laughed. "You said you wanted me."

"I didn't. I don't," she stumbled trying to wave him off.

"You most certainly did," he teased. "And you called me Benji. No one has ever called me that. What did we do, Irene? Did you kiss me?"

"No!" she denied hotly. "You kissed me!"

"Ah-ha!"

"Ohhh!" she squealed, realizing she'd exposed her secret. Hot tears of embarrassment stung her eyes. "I can't control what I dream about."

She felt the mattress compress as he sat next to her. "Irene, look at me."

"No."

"Irene," his voice gentled. "Would you feel better if I

told you I dreamt of you as well?"

She froze. "What?"

"Tis true."

She thought about his words for a moment. Had he really dreamt about her too? It didn't seem possible, more like the kind of thing you told a person in order to placate them. "You're lying," she accused as she peeked out from under the blanket.

"No." His eyes pierced into hers and she knew he told the truth. "It was a very strange dream. Very real. I held you in my arms as we said sweet things to each other and you called me Benji."

"Yes, she whispered. "You called me sweet girl."

All mischief fled his face. "Yes," he admitted.

"How can it be?" she asked. "How is it possible we dreamt the same dream?"

He stared at her, and for a moment Irene believed he would make the dream a reality and kiss her again. Then his cheeks flushed slightly and he stood up with a frown. "I do not know, but it seems obvious it was more than a dream."

"What does it mean?"

"I do not know that either." He stood and moved across the room. He ran a hand through his hair, leaving it wild in its wake. "I only know that the thing I want is wrong for so many reasons. Too many."

"But we had the same dream," Irene countered. "With all that's going on, it must mean something. It *must*."

"It means we are connected. How or why, I cannot say," he answered, his voice anguished. "But it matters naught. Two days ago I thought I loved Stella, and now I don't know what I feel. I seem to have lost my mind. How can I trust myself? Particularly when all I've ever known is dead and gone. I am dealing with all this the best I know how. Even if that were not enough, I will be gone in a few days. And we barely know each other, it makes no sense."

"No," she agreed, choking back her embarrassment. "Look, we have a lot to accomplish today and this kind of discussion can be a little draining. Let's not talk about this right now, Benji." Colored flooded her face at her inadvertent use of his nickname. "Benjamin!"

He turned to face her, his eyes stormy with pent up emotion. "You may call me Benji," he whispered hoarsely. "I do not mind."

They stared at each other across the room, before Benjamin took a step back toward the door. "I will leave you to prepare for your day."

He left the room and Irene fought back tears again.

"Ugh," she exclaimed in disgust. "I am so sick of crying. What is wrong with me?"

I believe I have an explanation, Holmes offered.

"I know exactly what your explanation is, and I don't want to hear it," she seethed. "Go away."

Holmes remained silent, and she went about her morning routine.

Half an hour later, she was dressed in jeans and a sweater and was heading out the front door with the professor in tow.

The courthouse was just across the square from the bookstore, so they were walking up the front steps within minutes.

"Public records are this way," Professor McGurty pointed down a hallway, leading the way for Irene. "I've spent some time here to study up on some of the local history, so I'm familiar with the clerk. Let me do the talking."

An older woman with graying hair piled in a bun on top of her head looked up when then entered the room. She sat behind a counter just a few feet from the door. Tall shelves packed with files and boxes filled the room behind her. Her face lit up when she saw the professor. "Professor!" she smiled.

Irene watched as Professor McGurty clasped the woman's hands in his own. "Lydia, how have you been? I'm almost surprised you're here today, what with all the chaos about town."

She gave him a look of disbelief. "You should know better. I haven't missed a day of work in fifteen years."

He chuckled. "True."

"Well," Lydia glanced at Irene then back at the professor. "I assume you're here on business. How can I help you?"

"We need to take a look at any records you have from the late 1800's," he answered. "Specifically around 1875. I'm looking for property records, business licenses, that kind of thing."

Lydia nodded. "Anything specific?"

"We need to find information on a company called SP Enterprises. And any land grabs involving Stone's Banking and Loan."

Irene stepped forward. "We also need to find any public information on a man named Benjamin Churchill and a woman named Stella Pennington. Possibly death certificates in September of that year."

Lydia stared at them for a moment. "What are you looking for specifically?"

Professor McGurty shook his head. "I'm not sure

you'd believe me if I told you."

She barked a laugh. "Try me."

Irene smiled. "Let's just say ghosts from the past have been popping up."

The professor laughed. "Yes, and we have a mystery to solve."

Lydia shrugged and opened the half door to let them behind the counter. "Big secret, eh? None of my business I suppose." She led them toward the back of the room. "The files you want are going to be back here."

They reached the farthest corner of the room where the boxes and files had begun to collect a bit of dust. "Sorry about the mess," Lydia apologized. "I don't get a lot of requests for these files. We mostly keep them for historical purposes."

She set up a step ladder so she could climb to the highest shelf, pulling down several boxes. "Here," she said, handing them to the professor. "These files cover 1850 to 1900. As you can see, we don't have a great deal from back then. Some of my predecessors were less than diligent in record keeping."

Professor McGurty took the boxes from her and set them on the floor. "Are they organized in a particular manner?"

She gave him an amused, albeit scathing look. "Of course. They're organized by year, and within each year you'll find records of births, marriages, deaths, et cetera in one section. Public records regarding businesses, real estate, et cetera are in another section." She waved a hand. "Everything is labelled."

Irene knelt down, pulled the lid off one of the boxes, and started rifling through the files. "Very nice," she commented, looking up at Lydia. "Very well organized. Thank you so much for your help."

"Bah," the older woman dismissed. "I've got nothing better to do right now. All the chaos in town means there hasn't been a soul in here today. I'll leave you to it, but let me know if I can help you with anything else."

Irene and the professor watched her walk back to her desk before they tackled the files. The professor pushed a box toward Irene. "This has all the business related files. Why don't you search for SP Enterprises and real estate sales? I'll take a look through the death certificates to see if we can find anything on Stella."

Irene nodded and began at the beginning of 1875. She'd found documentation of several real estate sales when the professor pulled a document from his box.

"Here's Benjamin," he declared. Irene took the document from him, studying it. Sure enough, it was his death certificate.

September 9th, 1875, she read. It was strange looking at the document when she knew he was back at her apartment waiting for her, a seemingly alive and vibrant man. She handed it back to Professor McGurty.

"I'll go make a copy of this," he told her, walking up to the front counter.

Irene continued searching the files in front of her, her heart sinking when she found the deed transferring ownership of property from Jedediah Hawkins to Stone's Banking and Loan. She set it aside and continued searching when a file labelled 'Business Licenses' caught her eye. She flipped to it and began searching through the few documents within.

Moments later, she found what she was looking for.

117

"Aha!" she cried, pulling the documents from the folder.

Her excitement, however, quickly turned to dismay as she read the document. "Professor," she called. "Professor, you have to see this!"

He came trotting back and took the paper from her, reading aloud. "SP Enterprises, sole proprietorship ..." He paled and glanced at Irene as he finished reading. "Stella ... Stella Pennington."

"SP Enterprises ... Stella Pennington," Irene breathed. "How on earth are we going to tell Benjamin?"

CHAPTER TWELVE

They sat outside the courthouse on the front steps, both of them reluctant to get back to the store and reveal what they'd learned to Benjamin.

The business license had been issued three months prior to Benjamin's death. How deeply Stella had been involved in the Hawkins' case was unclear, but one thing was certain: she knew more than she'd told Benjamin and she had lied to him.

The professor's usual enthusiasm seemed to have waned. "Perhaps you should be the one to tell him," he suggested. "I can go to the library and see if I can find any newspapers from 1875, then meet you back at the bookstore."

Irene shot him a look.

"I know, I know," he held up a hand. "I'm a chicken. I just don't know what to say to him. Besides, you have a connection to him. You can't deny it, I've seen the two of you together."

She nodded reluctantly, and hauled herself off the stairs to complete the unwelcome task. Waving goodbye to Professor McGurty, she began walking down the sidewalk to the bookstore, studying her shoes as she went.

Poor Benji, she thought. *How can I possibly tell him? He'll be devastated.*

You must simply lay out the facts as they are, Holmes came back. *He will not like it, but he will accept it. He will have no choice in the matter, particularly when he sees the business license.*

I know that, she countered with irritation. *But it will hurt him. I don't want to be the one to hurt him.*

Bah! Holmes dismissed. *Emotions matter naught. Only the truth.*

That's an awfully cold way of looking at things. Very unemotional.

Yes, as I've always been. You never objected before.

Stunned, she realized he was right. She'd always valued the coldly analytical mind of the detective, but suddenly it no longer seemed like a valuable trait. *I don't want that anymore,* she realized. *All it does is keep me away from people. And lonely. I'm tired of being lonely.*

Irene was so distracted by her sudden realization she didn't notice the person directly in front of her. Irene collided the woman and would have knocked her to the ground if her companion hadn't reached down and scooped her up. Something fell from the bag she was carrying, clinking loudly on the pavement.

Irene recognized Anika Butler, the owner of the antique store they now stood in front of. They'd never talked much, but Irene had always thought Anika was a quietly intelligent woman. Face flaming, she bowed down to pick up the item she'd knocked from Anika's bag. It was a bit of metal, not much bigger than the palm of her hand.

"Oh my God, I'm so sorry," she told Anika as she handed her the metal piece. "Are you okay?"

Anika reached for the proffered item. "Yes, I'm fine. I'm sorry, too … I wasn't watching where I was going."

"No," Irene insisted. "It was completely my … fault." She trailed off as she glanced back down at the metal piece in her hand.

Oh my God, it can't be.

Without realizing, she pulled the piece back so she could examine it more closely. Turning it over, she gasped as she looked down at the carved inscription, running a finger over the design. "This is it. I can't believe it."

Someone cleared their throat, and Irene startled. Her face flamed red as she realized she'd forgotten about the two people standing in front of her.

She looked up as a handsome man with dark brown skin stepped forward and tried to take the hilt from her. "Excuse me," he said. "We're going to need that back."

Irene pressed it against her chest to keep it out of his reach. "Please," she pleaded. "You don't understand. I have to have this. It's important."

A muscle ticked in his jaw as he clenched his teeth. "You're the one who doesn't understand. Do you know what you have there?"

Irene couldn't stop the wave of irritation that washed over her. Did he think she was an idiot? "Of course I do," she snapped. "This is a piece of the Star Anthame, isn't it? Don't try to tell me it isn't, I've seen drawings."

The man leaned forward, lowering his voice to a menacing pitch. "And I've had its blade buried between my ribs. This piece of it is the only chance I have left to break a curse cast over me by a witch. I'll be damned if I just let you walk away with it!"

Irene realized finally that the people standing in front of her were some of the people Flora had warned her about. They were searching for the pieces of the Star Anthame as well. She felt herself calm down a bit and decided to try to strike up a dialogue with the clearly desperate man.

"Would that witch happen to be named Priscilla?" she asked.

Anika stepped forward, placing a calming hand on the man's arm. "We've heard this witch has gone by many names over the past few centuries. Her name was Edith when she attacked Isaac and cursed him." She cocked her head to the side, studying Irene for a moment. "Listen, I don't know what you need the hilt for, but we need it to. Let's talk this out and maybe we can come to some kind of an agreement."

Irene studied the hilt again, reluctant to give it back, especially to the man who still looked furious. "She cursed him," she said thoughtfully. "And now he's stuck here in our time, but he needs to get back. I promised I would help him, and we need all three pieces of the relic to break the curse."

The man seemed to calm a bit at her words. "Who is this man?" he asked. "And why did he send you out alone to look for the pieces of the Anthame? Do you have any idea how dangerous it is for you to have even one part of the relic, or what the witch might do if she gets her hands on it?"

Irene shook her head in frustration. He still didn't understand. "He can't leave the bookstore." She waved a hand." Bah! It's hard to explain, but he's trapped between life and death, and can only maintain a corporeal form inside my shop. So you see, we don't have a choice. Someone has to do it, and I promised him I would be the one."

Anika glanced back and forth between them before whispering in Isaac's ear.

He sighed and flashed her a look of irritation before turning back to Irene. "How much time do you have?"

Irene hadn't known she was holding her breath until he spoke and she released it in a great whoosh. "I have until the end of the week, when the portal between worlds closes."

"Have you found any other piece of the relic?"

She nodded. "I have the blade."

The two stared at her with wide eyes.

"All I need now is the gem," Irene told them.

"Excellent," Anika gave her an approving look.

Isaac tried not to look impressed. "Very well, we will help you. But only after I have used the hilt to finish my mission. I have a witch waiting for me to bring her a part of the relic to use in breaking my curse. Once I have finished with it, I will deliver the hilt to you myself. All I ask, is that once you have assembled the Anthame and used it, you must destroy or disassemble it again. If it falls into the wrong hands, the consequences could be catastrophic. Can you do that for me?"

Irene nodded so hard her hair bounced. "Yes, I can do that. In fact, if I'm successful, we'll be able to destroy the power of the Anthame forever." She pointed to the markings on the hilt. "That's what this means. It's a prophecy telling how to destroy it."

They gaped at her for a moment until Isaac finally broke the silence. "This thing is just full of surprises," he quipped dryly, looking at the markings with new interest.

"One less thing to worry about," Anika quipped. "You concentrate on finding the gem. We'll make sure you have the hilt in plenty of time."

A thrill of victory ran through Irene and she smiled at them as she handed Anika the hilt. "Thank you. Thank you so much."

Isaac reached out a hand to her. "You're welcome. I apologize for being so rude, but it's difficult to know who to trust in times like these."

Irene took his hand, shaking it firmly. "Completely understandable," she told him. "I hope everything works out for you, Mr. ..."

"Parker," he answered. "Isaac Parker."

She smiled again. "Good luck, Isaac. You too, Anika." With one last glance at them, she continued toward the bookstore, nearly running in her eagerness to reach Benjamin and share the good news with him.

Two down, she thought. *One to go.*

CHAPTER THIRTEEN

Irene raced for the store, leaping up the stairs eagerly and bursting through the door. "Benjamin," she called, peering around store until she found him in the contemporary fiction room.

Once again, she caught him reading, although this time he didn't throw the book away from himself. Instead, he tried to hide it behind his back like an errant child with ill-gotten sweets.

She couldn't suppress her grin. "What is it this time?" she snickered, holding out a hand.

His face turned brilliant red and he handed her the book.

She looked at the cover and her snicker turned into a full on laugh. "Lola Whispers? A Knight's Tail? *Tail?*" she squeaked the last word. Opening the book, she began to read.

"His fingertip traced a line from her neck to her breasts. Vivian's breath caught when she felt his lips touch

the side of her neck. She tilted her head to the side and moaned.

"I want you," he whispered into her ear and pushed his body flush against hers so she couldn't help but feel the bulge of his erection through his jeans.

"Yes," she managed to nod, her voice ragged. "Right now." She wrapped her arms around his neck and savored the feel of his rippling muscles against her skin.

Jax needed no more invitation. He reached down and gripped her legs, hauling her up and holding her legs as her back pressed into the edge of the counter. She threw her head back and held onto his neck, linking her legs together so that he could undo his belt."

Irene stopped reading, she was laughing so hard. "Really, Benjamin. Why are you so fascinated with these books?"

His brown eyes turned stormy and he took a step toward her. "Haven't you ever felt like that?" he asked. "Like the woman in that story?"

Her breath caught in her throat. *Oh, yes, Benjamin, I have,* she thought weakly. *With you, on my kitchen floor. No man should be so beautiful. Or make my knees turn to jelly.*

She licked her lips nervously and his eyes followed the movement. His nostrils flared and when he met her gaze again, she saw something primal in them. Something … predatory.

He closed the distance between them, his hands snaking up to grip her shoulders, pulling her toward him. She dropped her purse on the floor. His lips brushed against hers as he spoke. "How about now, Irene?" he whispered. "Is it funny now?"

Irene whimpered and a moment later he crushed his lips against hers.

All rational thought fled her mind and she threw her arms around his neck, pulling him down to her, trying to get closer. His tongue swept along the edge of her lips before plunging in to taste her.

She moaned, as he wrapped his arms around her, crushing her breasts against his hard chest. His mouth moved down her throat leaving a blazing trail behind. "Benji," she gasped.

He turned her, walking her backward until her back was against the wall. "Why can't I stay away from you?" he muttered against her throat.

His words thrilled her, emboldening her. "For the same reason I can't stay away from you," she whispered back.

"Irene," he groaned, grasping her hands in his and pressing his body against hers.

She had nowhere to go and could only stand helplessly as he ground against her, creating a tension low in the pit of her belly. She felt a dampness between her legs and for a moment, she saw stars.

Her head fell back wantonly. "I've never felt like this before," she whispered.

"Neither have I," he responded. "I have never wanted a woman as I want you. I have never found myself thinking of a woman as much as I think of you." He pulled away a little, frowning. "Not even Stella."

His former fiancée's name hit Irene like a bucket of ice water and sucked in a breath, turning her face away from his. Stella. How could she have forgotten? How could she let herself get so distracted? And how was she going to tell him about SP Enterprises? In her excitement over the hilt, she'd forgotten about her original task for the day and the horrible discovery she'd made.

Benjamin sensed the change in her demeanor and let go of her hands. He stepped back. "Once again I find myself apologizing for being so forward."

"No, Benji," she gasped. "I- I'm not upset about that."

"What's wrong? Is it about Armin?" He frowned. "It's Stella, isn't it?" He peered around her. "Where is the professor? Did you discover who was behind SP Enterprises?"

She looked away. "I- yes. Yes I did."

"Well?" he waited for a moment and when she didn't answer, he leveled her with a probing gaze. "What is it? What did you find out?"

Irene couldn't seem to find her voice, instead, she pulled the copies of the business license out of her purse and silently handed it to him.

"What is this …" Benjamin trailed off as he examined the document. A moment later, his eyes shot to hers, the blood draining from his face. "This can't be."

Irene winced a little at the denial. She wanted to comfort him, but she didn't know what to say. Finally, she managed to choke out two words. "I'm sorry."

"No!" he said sharply, shaking his head. "How can it be? Stella never would have done such a thing. She- she was a good woman."

Irene just watched him.

"Maybe she took over the company after she lost me," he offered hopefully.

"You died in September," Irene murmured. "Look at

the date on the license. It's dated June. Before you died."

He looked as she instructed, before staring at her again with clenched teeth. A muscle ticked in his jaw and Irene felt tears pooling in her eyes. She wanted to go to him, hold him and comfort him, but he seemed so angry she hesitated.

A moment later he let out an almost savage snarl as he crumpled up the paper and tossed it across the room. "Damn the devil!"

He paced the room, his hands tearing at his hair. "How? How is this possible? How could she stand right there and listen to me as I talked about some god damned mystery company that she *owned the whole time!*" His fist slammed into the wall along the doorway, and the cherry framed Beeton's Christmas Annual on the other side jumped and fell to the floor, the UV glass shattering as the frame broke apart.

Irene cried out, rushing across the room and falling to her knees. She carefully picked pieces of glass off the annual to avoid tearing or scratching it, and removed it. She stroked a finger over the words on the page, reading the words to the Sherlock Holmes story. Tears slipped down her cheeks and she looked up." Oh, Benji, how could you?" she admonished quietly.

His anger seemed to melt away and he dropped down beside her. "I'm sorry. Truly I am." He watched her tenderly holding the magazine. "This document is important to you, isn't it?"

She nodded. "Yes."

He groaned. "Which makes my thoughtlessness even worse. I would never want to hurt you, and yet I have through my lack of control."

"I know you didn't do it on purpose," she whispered.

"Is it still intact?"

She examined before nodding. "Yes. I just need to keep it in a safe place and get a new frame for it."

Benjamin helped her to her feet and she went to put the magazine in the safe behind the counter. When it was securely locked up, she fetched a broom and dustpan. Benjamin took them from her.

"Let me do this," he insisted. "I made the mess, it's only right that I should clean it up."

She watched as he swept the bits of glass into the pan.

"Where is the professor?" he asked as he worked.

"He went to the library to see if he could find any old newspapers with information we might find relevant." She shrugged. "Mostly I think he wanted to avoid the conversation we just had."

Benjamin frowned. "I suppose I understand that."

She searched his face for a moment. "Are you okay? I was so worried about telling you. I just didn't want to hurt you."

He squeezed his lips together, his brow furrowing. "I will be all right," he answered slowly.

"Perhaps she had a good reason?" Irene proposed as she sat on her stool behind the counter. "Maybe she was owner of SP Enterprises in name only and someone else was behind it."

He shook his head. "Even if that were the case, which I doubt, she still knew about the company. When I mentioned it to her, why didn't she confess her part in it?"

Irene opened her mouth to offer an explanation, but closed it again when she could find none.

"Exactly," Benjamin stated. "No, it's clear she was

deceiving me all along."

"You must be devastated."

He dumped a dustpan full of glass into a waste bin before putting it and the broom away. He came back to the counter, leaning against it. "I feel betrayed, yes, and shocked that Stella was able to conceal her true nature from me, but somehow it is my pride that stings the most. My heart …" he trailed off as he captured Irene's gaze.

Her mouth went dry. "Yes?" she rasped.

He reached across the counter and took her hand in his. Her skin tingled where he touched her. "It seems my heart was never truly hers to begin with, else how could I feel for you as I do?"

Irene inhaled slightly before closing her eyes as she attempted to control her emotions. "Benjamin," she began to protest.

"I know," he interrupted, letting go of her hand. She opened her eyes to look at him again. "If we can ever find all the pieces of the knife, I will be gone in just a few days. Either way, I will be gone. It is an impossible situation."

The knife!

Irene realized she'd forgotten to tell him about the hilt.

He did distract you in a most ungentlemanly manner, Holmes berated. *How very crass.*

Shut up, she told him. *I liked it.*

"Actually," she said out loud, giving Benjamin a sheepish grin. "I have news on that front. I found the hilt."

His jaw dropped open. "What? When? Where? How?"

Irene chuckled and help up a hand. "Slow down, one question at a time."

"Can I see it?"

"Well," she bit down on her lip a little, trying to decide where to start. "I don't actually have it on me."

His nose wrinkled adorably with confusion. "Where is it?"

"Remember when I told you that the witch said we weren't the only people looking for the Star Anthame?" She waited, continuing when he nodded. "Well, I ran into Anika Parker, the owner of the antique store here in the square. Literally ran into her. Almost knocked her over. She dropped something when I crashed into her, and I couldn't believe it when I picked it up because there it was, the hilt."

"You gave it back to them?" His eyes were wide with incredulity. "How could you do that?"

"They need it too, Benjamin," she reasoned. "And we talked it out. They know what our time frame is and agreed to bring it to me when they were done with it. Apparently they only need the hilt."

"Do you trust this woman, this Anika?"

Irene thought for a moment. "I don't really know her that well but I trust her as much as I trust anyone, I suppose. Other than the professor. I've helped him with materials for his classes since I opened the bookstore."

"You consider him a friend, then?"

"Well," Irene plucked at her bottom lip with her teeth. "We've always been friendly, but this is the first time we've done anything outside of a work scenario. I'd say we're more colleagues than friends." She reddened. "I like him very much, though."

Benjamin studied her for a moment, and when he spoke, his voice was gentle. "Who are your friends, Irene?"

She turned away. "I- I don't really have any friends, I guess. Acquaintances, but no one I'd consider close."

"Why?"

Tears threatened again, and she sighed. *I am so sick of crying,* she thought. She kept that thought to herself as she looked down at her hands twisting together nervously. "I don't know. I've just always been more comfortable with my books, and when I opened the bookstore, it just became easier to exist here. I've been alone most of my life, or almost alone."

He reached out and placed his fingers under her chin, lifting her face so he could capture her gaze. "What happened to your family?"

"You know about my father," she choked out. "My mother died when I was sixteen and I came to Saint's Grove to live with my aunt. She died after I turned eighteen. I have no other family."

"And why did you never make any friends?"

She lifted her shoulders. "I was shy, I guess. And ..." She thought about how she'd developed so early, her figure had turned to that of a woman's long before she was ready, and how she had withdrawn as a means of avoiding unwanted attention.

"What?" he pressed. "What happened? You're an intelligent woman. Thoughtful, funny, warm. Not to mention the most beautiful woman I've ever seen."

She blushed at his words, her heart beating wildly. It thrilled her to know he thought she was beautiful, but she was so used to avoiding men that it made her nervous too. "That's part of the problem," she whispered.

Benjamin cocked his head, his brow wrinkling. "I

don't understand."

Irene felt like her face might burst into flames. "Do you know what it's been like? To have men-" She swallowed, trying to find the nerve to tell him. "To have men look at you like you're not even a person. Can you imagine someone like me living in this body? I've looked like this pretty much since I was fourteen. It was horrible." She shuddered and her voice dropped to a whisper. "They thought I was older than I was, and would try to talk to me, sometimes touch me. I- I didn't know what to do, so I just withdrew into my books."

Benjamin came around the counter and took her in his arms. "I'm so sorry you had to go through that."

Irene pressed her face against his chest, reveling in his warmth and smell. *Why does he have to go?* She thought suddenly. *Why can't he stay with me? I only just found him, and now the only man I could ever love is going to leave.*

Love? Came Holmes incredulous voice. *My dear Miss Bell, you barely know the man, not to mention love is a fallacy. It is merely an amalgam of genetically pleasing physical traits and hormones.*

You're wrong, she argued. *I might have agreed with you three days ago, but now I know you're wrong. I'm not prone to flights of fancy or ridiculous notions.*

My dear, we are all animals and therefore susceptible to biology, at least once or twice in our lives. Even I once found a woman to admire. Of course, it was based on more than base animal attraction.

That's not what this is!

Methinks the lady doth protest too much.

Go away!

"Irene?"

She realized Benjamin had been talking to her, and she looked up at him, blushing again. "I feel like I'm always blushing or crying around you," she muttered.

His mouth quirked as he held back a laugh.

"Don't laugh at me," she pulled away from him, her nostrils flaring slightly with irritation.

Her response only made matters worse, and his grin widened as he snorted slightly.

The next thing she knew, they were exploding with laughter together.

"Damn you for laughing!" she wheezed. "It's not funny!"

"Oh yes it is," he retorted. "Because I feel the same way."

"You haven't cried once in front of me," she giggled.

"No, but how many times have you caught me reading those perverse novels?" he snickered. "I had no idea my face could burn so hotly with embarrassment."

At that moment, Professor McGurty walked in, the sound of the door startling both of them so they jumped. Both Benjamin and Irene dissolved into another fit of laughter while the professor stood by, watching them with bemusement.

"I feel like I've walked into the middle of a private joke," he uttered, shaking his head. Irene opened her mouth to explain, but he held up a hand. "No, no, don't explain. There are more important things going on." He pulled several papers out of his jacket pocket.

Benjamin and Irene sobered quickly.

Benjamin spoke first. "What did you find out?"

The professor studied him for a moment. "Did she tell

you?"

"About SP Enterprises?" Benjamin asked. Professor McGurty nodded. "Yes, she did. Stella was the sole proprietor."

The professor's lips pressed together in a grim line. "Not for long she wasn't." He handed over the papers.

Benjamin studied them, his expression growing darker and darker with every word until an expression Irene had never seen on his face graced his handsome features. It was an expression of pure rage. "That bitch," he snarled.

"Indeed," Professor McGurty nodded. "And a cold hearted one at that."

"What?" Irene asked fearfully. "What is it?"

Benjamin turned stormy eyes in her direction. "It's Stella," he snarled. "And she must have been behind everything. Including my murder."

CHAPTER FOURTEEN

I rene's mouth fell open. "What do you mean?"

Benjamin's fingers curled around the papers, crushing them in his palm before handing them to Irene. She smoothed them out and began reading.

The first piece of paper was a copy of wedding announcement announcing the marriage of Stella Pennington and Marlon Stone on October 31st, 1875. Irene looked up at Benjamin. "But that's less than two months after you …" she trailed off as his already dark expression turned murderous.

"Yes," he responded, carefully enunciating every word. "For a woman who purportedly loved me, she was able to move passed her grief quite speedily."

Irene flipped to the next page, her eyes widening as she read the article. "Stone's Banking and Loan Merges with SP Enterprises, November 5th, 1875," she read the headline aloud. The article itself seemed innocuous. However, knowing what she knew, a very clear picture of what had happened all those years ago began to form as she read it to herself.

A longtime pillar of the Saint's Grove community has merged with a relative newcomer enterprise to create a brand new corporation in an attempt to bring new business and new opportunities to the entire town.

Stone's Banking and Loan has joined forces with SP Enterprises, a little known company with big dreams. And as it turns out, roots within the Saint's Grove community. Stella Stone, nee Pennington, the audacious and ambitious daughter of Martin Pennington of Pennington Dry Goods, formed SP Enterprises in an attempt to bring youth and vigor to our little hamlet.

"I wanted to help the town I love so much," she told this reporter. "However, it became clear to me quite early on that my female sensibilities were just not up to par for the task, so I decided to enlist the aid of my dear husband."

Stone's Banking and Loan will naturally stay open and ready to help all the good citizens of Saint's Grove. They will, however, be putting their efforts into their combined interests, the first being the new corporation of Penstone Mining.

Penstone Mining has purchased several vacant plots of land along the base of the Blue Ridge Mountains where they will begin mining for gold.

"There's a deep pocket in those mountains we found quite by accident," the lovely Mrs. Stone said. "This enterprise will bring an entire new industry to Saint's Grove, as well as a number of jobs. I'm grateful for the opportunity to give back to the town I love so much."

Penstone Mining breaks ground in the spring. In the

meantime, those who are hoping to secure a position in this exciting new venture can apply in person at their new office next to Stone's Banking and Loan.

"We want to hire as many locals as possible," Mrs. Stone told this reporter with a sunny smile. "We hope someday the entire town will be as fortunate and prosperous as we have been."

The entire town should count themselves lucky to have civic-minded pillars of the community like Marlon and Stella Stone.

Irene looked at Benjamin with shocked eyes. "She knew all along."

"Of course she did," he retorted. "She stood in my office listening to me go on about Jed Hawkins and how I wanted to save his farm from the evil bank. They must have sat back and had a good laugh at my expense. What a fool I am," he finished bitterly.

Irene put a sympathetic hand on his shoulder. "Not a fool," she told him softly. "You trusted her. And she did everything she could to ensure that you did."

"Perhaps," he answered, his jaw clenching. "What I truly don't understand is that I courted her long before all of this. Long before Hawkins came to see me, several months before she formed SP Enterprises. Why would she start up with me at all if she was in collusion with Stone? Why not just marry him to begin with? Why involve me at all?"

Irene motioned them to follow her upstairs so they could have lunch, and the three of them fell into silence as they pondered his questions.

Once upstairs, Irene spoke first. "We know you were cursed when you were stabbed with the Star Anthame.

And we know you interfered with the witch Priscilla's plans somehow. We also know she has survived by possessing people through the centuries, jumping from body to body. What if," she reasoned slowly as she poured canned soup into a pot, "Stella wasn't Stella anymore?"

The two men stared at her.

"Of course!" The professor snapped his fingers. "Stella was possessed by the witch. Somehow, somewhere, Priscilla took possession of her body. She kept up the ruse of being in love with you," he pointed at Benjamin. "Then proceeded to make herself the richest woman Saint's Grove has ever seen."

"How do you know that?" Benjamin asked.

"Because Penstone Mining almost killed this town," Irene answered grimly before the professor had a chance to open his mouth. "And everyone in town knows the story of how the original owners ravaged the land, stripping it of every scrap of gold they could find before selling the company and moving to Charleston. The company would have failed completely if they hadn't found coal a couple years later."

"The original owners took every dime," the professor added as he helped Irene prepare tuna sandwiches. "There wasn't anything left, and so many people worked for the company that when they took the money and ran, the entire town plummeted into a depression that took years to recover from."

Irene turned to Professor McGurty. "I had no idea the original owners were Marlon and Stella Stone. Did you?"

He shook his head. "No, and I've studied some of the history of that time. I was under the impression that it was owned by a couple named Armin and Stella Churchill …"

He trailed off as he stared at Benjamin. He struck himself on the forehead. "My God! How could I have been so stupid! I never made the connection until now."

"My brother?" Benjamin exclaimed, his face darkening with rage. "She married my brother?"

"It would appear so," Professor McGurty nodded.

"It makes sense," Irene piped up as she handed each of the men a bowl of steaming hot vegetable soup and a plated sandwich. "She kills Benji, marries Stone and merges the businesses, kills him and marries Armin so she has a patsy. Who knows what happened to him after they ran off with all the money."

"Yes," agreed the professor as he blew softly on a spoonful of soup. "No one ever heard from them again after they left town." He gave Benjamin a sorrowful look. "I'm sorry, son. I don't know that we'll ever find out what happened to your brother. At least, not in the time we have left."

Benjamin's brow wrinkled. "Patsy?"

"A chump," explained the professor. "Sucker, easy mark, a dupe, a fool, a schmuck."

Benjamin pressed his lips together so tightly they seemed to disappear for a moment. "We have to take her out," he snarled. "We can't let her keep going on like this, destroying the lives of everyone she comes in contact with."

"We have to help you crossover," Irene protested.

He slammed a hand on the table causing his bowl to jump and soup to slosh over the side. "I don't care about me anymore!" he gritted. "This is more important than me. *She has to be stopped.*"

"You're right," Irene agreed. "We can't let her con-

tinue. So much destruction, so many lives lost." She shuddered as she glanced at Benjamin. "I'm so sorry about
your brother."

"But how?" asked the professor. "How do we stop
her?"

"Well," Irene thought while she took a bite of her
sandwich. She chewed slowly before answering. "We
know we're not the only ones looking for the Star Anthame or the witch. And we're so close to having all the
pieces of the blade now that we know where the hilt is."

Professor McGurty stopped eating and stared at them
with large eyes. "What? Since when?"

Irene and Benjamin looked sheepishly at each other.

"We were distracted with your news," Irene told the
professor. "I ran into Anika Butler from the antique store
and a man named Isaac Parker who claimed to have been
cursed by a witch named Edith. Pricilla from a different
time, I'm assuming," she added. "They had the hilt and
agreed to give it to me after they break the curse."

Professor McGurty nodded as he digested the new information. "And since it stands to reason Lisa from the
museum is possessed by Priscilla, her brother will be looking for a way to save her, or purge the witch from her
body. If that's even possible."

"Yes," Irene nodded. "It seems we may have allies."

"Do you really think they'll help us?" Benjamin
asked.

"I'm betting they have as big a bone to pick with her
as you do," she answered. "And Isaac was clearly furious
when he talked about Edith. He'll want to take her out in
the worst way, I'm sure of it."

"Well, then," declared the professor as he took a large

bite of his sandwich. "I think it's time to pay our friends a visit."

"Yes, Benjamin agreed. "However, I think you have another chore that's more important."

"What's that?"

"The witch has powers that have kept her alive for hundreds of years as she moves from body to body. How do you kill someone like that?"

Irene opened her mouth to answer, then shut it as she realized he was right. They had no idea how to stop her.

"He's right," she said to the professor. "We need to go see Flora. If anyone knows how to kill the witch, it'll be her."

Benjamin shooed Irene and Professor McGurty out the door after lunch, insisting he would clean up.

"You told me that in this age, men have become domestics." He grinned at the professor. "Besides, I have nothing else to do with my time."

"You could find another book to read," Irene suggested. "Maybe one without a half-naked woman on the cover?"

The professor turned away, rubbing his upper lip while Benjamin arched a brow at her. "Aren't you a clever girl?" he scoffed, swatting at her as she scurried out the front door.

She snickered as the professor caught up with her and they walked across the square. They didn't talk much as they trekked toward the outskirts of town and Flora's home, but after several sidelong and seemingly mirthful glances from the professor, Irene finally broke the silence.

"What?" she demanded mildly. "You've been giving me those looks since we left the bookstore. Clearly you have something on your mind. What is it?"

He glanced at her again, as if he were looking for something specific in her expression before he answered. "You're in love with him."

"In love?" she parroted. "What are you talking about?"

"Don't deny it, young lady. I've been in love. I know what it looks like, and I see it in you when you look at Benjamin."

Holmes seemed to agree with him. *His powers of observation are impeccable.*

Irene ignored the detective and answered Professor McGurty instead. "Don't be ridiculous. Love? I barely know the man."

He smiled knowingly. "Time has nothing to do with it. Love can happen in an instant. One minute you're living your life and the next you're living your life for those moments when you can see that special person again. Or touch them again. Or even make them smile again."

She shook her head. "I- you're wrong, Professor. I like him, certainly, but love?"

"Yes, my dear, love." He nodded emphatically. "And what's more, I believe he's in love with you too."

Excitement sparked her senses and she spoke without thinking. "Really? You think so?" She reddened as she heard the eagerness in her voice, realizing she'd given herself away.

His expression softened. "Yes. It's obvious how he feels about you. You should tell him how you feel."

Irene bit her lip, afraid to respond, and Holmes took the moment to speak up again.

You are aware, my dear, that as a base biological function, attraction fades? Please Miss Bell, it's time you rejoined me in the arena of sensibility and logic.

But if he loves me...

And what if he does? In four days he will be gone forever and you will be heartbroken.

Maybe there's a way to keep him here.

Perhaps. However, are you certain he wants to stay? And if you could find a way to make that happen, what would he do? He's from a time long past. He isn't made for your world.

It was a good question, she realized, one that she had no answer for. What *would* Benjamin do if he were able to stay?

No, the detective was right. She ought to keep her distance from him, if only to protect herself.

She sighed and glanced at the professor as they climbed the dirt road toward Flora's house. "What good would telling him do? All that can happen is we'll both be hurt when he's gone. It's better to leave things as they are."

"Oh, certainly the wisest course of action," Professor McGurty agreed. "But I can tell you from personal experience that the moments we remember the most in life aren't the times when we were most prudent. The best memories I have are those times when I made decidedly unwise decisions." He stopped walking and grasped her hand in his, his eyes slightly pleading. "Safe is not always better, my dear."

Irene felt tears forming in her eyes as she looked into his, and she nodded briefly. "Perhaps you're right," she managed to choke out. "You've certainly given me something to think about."

He smiled slightly and let go of her hands so he could pat her on the shoulder. "Good girl."

They continued down the road, finally reaching Flora's.

This time the seer was outside tending to an herb garden along the fence. She looked up when they approached.

She nodded slightly in Irene's direction. "I knew I'd see you again," she muttered before glancing at Professor McGurty. "I didn't expect to see you, though. How are you Mycroft?"

Irene gaped at the professor. How had she never known his first name? And how strange was it that he shared the unusual moniker with that of Sherlock Holmes' brother?

"Mycroft?" she squeaked. "Your name is Mycroft? As in 'Mycroft Holmes?'"

"Oh yes," he answered with a pleasant expression. "My father was a huge fan of Doyle's work. You're familiar, I assume?"

She could only gape at him and nod, stunned by the coincidence.

"Yes, well," Flora interrupted, her voice tinged with annoyance. "This is all very fascinating, but why don't we get down to business. Why are you here?"

Irene blinked, then glanced at the tiny woman. "Sorry. I just- I'm sorry," she concluded lamely.

"My dear, Flora," Professor McGurty said, flashing

her a smile. "I don't remember you being so cross thirty years ago."

To Irene's astonishment, Flora blushed slightly. "I apologize, Mycroft. I've had a lot of visitors the last few days. My patience has been running thin."

The thin man took her hand in his, squeezing it slightly as Irene watched them open-mouthed. "Yes, I imagine that would be stressful. You're forgiven, my dear."

Flora smiled prettily at him. "Why don't you come inside and I'll make a bit of tea?"

Again, Irene could only gape as she followed the pair inside.

It seems to me, Holmes observed, *that you and the ghost are not the only ones experiencing an infatuation.*

For the first time in days, Irene agreed with the detective.

Once inside and settled with a cup of herbal tea, Flora settled her gaze on Irene. "Now, tell me child. Why are you here again?"

"We've learned a great deal in the last few days," she answered. "We know why Benjamin was murdered, that the witch Priscilla had possessed his fiancée, and that she's behind a great many terrible things that have happened in Saint's Grove. The more we learn, the worse it gets."

Flora rolled her eyes. "Of course it is. Like I told you, she's an evil witch. The evilest."

Irene suppressed a giggle at her choice of words. "Yes, well, as much as we want to help Benjamin crossover, he's determined that we need to stop her."

"Stop her?" Flora inquired, her eyes widening. "You don't mean what I think you mean, do you?"

Professor McGurty nodded. "We have to stop her no

matter what. Kill her if needed. That's why we've come to you. If anyone will know what to do, it's you."

"Yes," Irene agreed, leaning toward the other woman with urgency. "How do we kill someone who can just jump from one body to the next? How do we stop her?"

Flora sighed and lifted her teacup to her lips, blowing softly and taking a sip before she answered. "It is through the immense power of the Star Anthame that she has gained the ability to survive through the centuries, and it is through that same power she will be defeated. The body she currently possesses must be pierced through the heart with the Anthame. Fully assembled, mind you."

Professor McGurty frowned, running a hand through his sparse hair. "We think the possessed person is Lisa Hunter from the museum. I don't want to see any harm come to her."

Flora put down her teacup. "The blade will recognize the presence of Priscilla inside her. As long as you are correct and Lisa truly is possessed by Priscilla, she won't be harmed. Priscilla will be purged from Lisa's body and she will disappear into the netherworld once and for all." She snorted. "And good riddance to bad rubbish, too."

Irene ran a finger around the edge of her teacup. "You make it sound so simple."

Flora snorted again. "Simple? There's nothing simple about it. Priscilla is as intelligent as she is evil. She'll see you coming from a mile away."

"Then how do we get to her?"

"She needs a reason to come to you," Flora answered as she took a sip of tea. She put the cup down and ran her fingers over the arm of her chair, seemingly lost in thought. "She has a habit of cursing the men she falls in love with." She grimaced. "Or whatever twisted emotions she dares call love. I doubt she would know the difference. She may have loved your ghost once upon a time, but she didn't hesitate to have him killed. And she's moved on since then."

"To who?" Irene scoffed. "How could she move on from Benjamin?"

Flora and Professor McGurty stared at her, and she felt her face flame.

Most revealing, my dear, Holmes seemed to tease her.

She ignored him as she tried to ignore the knowing smile crossing the professor's face. She turned to Flora. "You seem to know who she's moved onto."

The witch nodded. "Yes. A man named Isaac Parker. She's been obsessed with him for over a century."

Irene exchanged a look with the professor. "I met him this morning," she told Flora. "He was with Anika Butler from the antique store." She leaned toward the other woman, her voice taking on a tinge of excitement. "They have the hilt to the Star Anthame and are willing to let me use it."

Flora's eyes widened. "They found it? Well, I'll be seeing the two of them very soon." She seemed to be talking to herself, so Irene waited until the petite woman looked at her again. "That only leaves two pieces for you to find. Any leads yet?"

Irene sat straighter and smiled. "We found the blade yesterday."

Flora's eyes seemed to widen even further before she relaxed a little and sat back in her chair. She closed her eyes, humming a bit. A hint of a smile crossed her face. "Yes," she murmured. "The time is here. The last piece will be delivered from the past and the Anthame will once again be fully assembled. It will spell her defeat. Love will destroy her and the power of the Athame will be broken. The time is here. Those who have been trapped will finally be free and those who are seeking will finally find. The time is here."

She shuddered, her tiny body arching in her chair before she sank back and sighed. A moment later, she opened tired eyes and smiled kindly at Irene. "Don't worry, child. Fate has already decided. Everything will work out exactly as it is meant to."

Irene bit her lip, nodding as she remembered Benjamin saying almost the exact same words to her, but hearing it from Flora gave it a sort of legitimacy. Irene couldn't help believing her that fate had, indeed, decided.

Professor McGurty leaned toward Flora and took her hand in his. "Are you well?" he asked, concern etched across his features. "That, vision or whatever you call it seems to have exhausted you."

She gave his hand a gentle squeeze. "I will be fine. In fact, I will be more than fine. This event is finally going to give me the peace I've been searching for," she told them with an enigmatic expression. "I am looking forward to it."

The professor pressed her for explanations, but she waved him off, insisting they head back to town before it grew dark. "You don't want to be walking this lonely road once the moon rises. Too bad the roads to town are still blocked in some places."

Irene and the professor glanced at each other, realizing other dangers lurked about in town and the surrounding woods. It was not safe to be out and about at night as long as the rift was open.

"I think we should be off," he told her.

Flora stood to see them off. "Wait," she told them, opening a box on an end table. She drew out two items, what looked like cross-shaped lockets on silver chains. "Take these and wear them for protection. I fear you will not make it home before dark."

They took the chains and fastened them around their necks. "What are they?" Irene asked as she tucked it into her blouse.

Flora waved a hand. "Just a charm, although they are both made of silver so they should offer some protection from various creatures." She grasped the professor's hand again. "You know, Mycroft, when this is all over, you should come by for a cup of tea."

He studied her, his face softening a bit. "I think I might just do that. And maybe you'll let me take you dancing one night at the Mountaintop Bar and Grill. They play some good blues sometimes."

Her face lit up and she nodded. "I think I would like that."

Irene watched the exchange open-mouthed until Flora rolled her eyes. "What's wrong with you, girl? You think old people don't enjoy a little one on one time as much as you and your ghost lover?"

Irene flushed a brilliant red. "I- I-"

The older couple snickered and finally the professor took pity on her, leading her out the door. "I'll give you a ring," he called back to Flora as they left. "And thank you for the charms."

"You better," she called back. "And you're welcome."

CHAPTER FIFTEEN

I rene and Professor McGurty were only halfway back to town when the sun began to set. She watched anxiously as it began to dip behind the Blue Ridge Mountains, the sky an amalgam of reds and oranges and golds settling on top of the azure haze that gave the mountains their name.

"Professor," she asked anxiously. "If we need to go out tomorrow, do you think we can take your truck? At least, as much as we can?"

He patted her shoulder. "Of course, my dear."

They walked a little further and she thought again about his name. "Professor, you said your father was a Sherlock Holmes fan and that's why he named you Mycroft. Did you know my family is descended from the inspiration for Holmes?"

He smiled. "Yes, I did. It was one of the reasons your father and I became friends. I knew him when I was in college. We went to school together."

"You did?" she squeaked. "Why didn't you ever tell me?"

He stopped walking and fixed her with a leveled gaze. "Irene, this is the first time since you came to live with your aunt that you let anyone into your world. Every interaction we've ever had you've managed to keep professional and business-like. Even when you turned eighteen and started college. You never made friends and you kept everyone at arm's length."

"I know," she nodded. "I just didn't know how to talk to people."

They started walking again, the sun inching lower and lower behind the mountains.

"Did you know my mother?" she continued.

He shrugged. "I met her once, but I wouldn't say I knew her. Your father brought her home shortly after they were married."

"What was she like?"

"Oh, she seemed shy, but she had a quietly wry sense of humor and the sunniest smile. And she smiled a lot. I think she was terribly in love with your father, and he with her."

Irene shook her head, trying to imagine her mother smiling all the time, let alone having a sense of humor. "It sounds like someone completely different from the woman I knew. I wish I'd known her then. I think part of her died when my father disappeared and she never really recovered."

"Yes," he responded gently. "Perhaps that is the reason you have never let yourself get close to someone."

Indignation rose inside her. "Maybe I have a right to be a little scared," she snapped lightly. "Everyone I've ever cared about at all has died."

"Everyone?" he questioned. "Who is everyone?"

"My father, my mother, Aunt Caroline."

"Irene, that's three people," he countered. "You've limited yourself to caring about three people in your entire life. You do understand that death is part of living, don't you? We all lose people."

She felt tears rising in her eyes, and she struggled to contain them. "You don't know what it was like, watching my mother wither away year after year. By the time she died, she rarely spoke, smiled even less, and I can't remember the last time she laughed. She was a shell." She shook her head with vehemence. "I just can't bear the thought of letting myself love someone so much that I lose myself as she did."

"Irene," he replied with force. "You are not your mother. Just because she let herself stop living when your father left, doesn't mean the same thing will happen to you. You have more fire and spark than she did even before your father disappeared. I don't believe you would ever lose yourself like that."

She thought of Benjamin and how it felt to kiss him and hold him close to her. She pictured the concern on his face when he worried over her venturing out to look for the Anthame or to find information. She tried to imagine the end of the week when the rift closed and how she would feel when he disappeared from her life forever. "I don't know," she whispered as a tear slipped down her cheek. "I'm beginning to see how powerful falling in love can be."

"It is very powerful," he agreed. "And yes, it can be painful. But a life without love, without a connection to

others is no life at all. You've been going through the mo-
tions, but you haven't really been living. I know it's cliché,
but there is great truth behind the saying that it's better to
have loved and lost than never to have loved at all."

Only a sliver of the sun remained, lining the horizon.
The trees that had previously cast their shadows along the
road gave way to darkness as the moon climbed the sky
opposite of the sun. "Maybe," she responded. "But-"

Suddenly a howl filled the air, echoing around them.
They both froze for a moment, glancing at each other fearfully.

Irene felt the blood drain from her face. "Werewolf,"
she whispered.

"Yes," the professor whispered back, beads of sweat
popping up along his forehead. "We better hurry. We're
still about a quarter mile outside of town."

They hurried down the road, both silent with worry.
They had just come around the last bend of the road that
obscured the night lights of Saint's Grove when another
howl rang out. This one was even closer than the last, and
without a word to each other, they picked up their pace to
a brisk jog.

Moments later, Irene heard a galloping footfall hitting
the dirt-packed road behind them. "Professor," she gasped,
reaching for his hand to urge him into a run.

He glanced over his shoulder and his fingers tightened painfully around hers. "Oh, dear God," he wheezed
as they sprinted down the road.

Despite her better judgement, she followed his gaze.
Terror gripped her and she wished she hadn't looked. Several hundred yards behind them a huge gray wolf streaked
toward them under the moonlight. Its eyes seemed intent

on her, and as she met its gaze, it threw back its head, never breaking stride as it howled again. Snarling, it closed the distance.

Irene turned back focusing on the road. She could see the edge of town, perhaps a hundred yards away, and irrationally told herself if they made it to the city limits they would be safe. *Surely it won't come into town.*

My dear, what makes you think that? Holmes chimed in. *You saw the wolf in the town square. Nothing will prevent it from entering town. You cannot outrun it.*

"Shut up!" she wheezed.

"Who- who are you talking to?" the professor panted.

She ignored the question, pulling on his hand. "Hurry!" she urged him.

As they crossed the edge of town, Irene looked over her shoulder again. The wolf was only a few feet away and it growled with ferocity as she met its gaze just before it leapt for her. She screamed as it hit her with the force of a freight train, knocking her to the ground.

It's powerful jaws snapped, mere inches from her face, and she screamed again, trying to push it off her.

"The charm," yelled Professor McGurty as he leapt on top of the wolf. "Use the charm!"

The wolf roared, rearing up on its hind legs and throwing the professor off its back. The distraction gave Irene enough time to yank the chain off her neck before the wolf settled on all four paws again. It snarled, opening its huge jaws to expose wicked looking teeth. Irene took that moment to shove the charm directly into its mouth.

Instantly, the wolf recoiled, falling onto its back next to her as it howled in agony.

Irene scooted away from it, heaving painfully, never

taking her eyes off the creature as it writhed and wailed.

A moment later, a hand grasped hers, yanking her to her feet. She shrieked until she saw it was the professor, and then she wrapped her arms around him. "You're all right," she sobbed.

"Yes," he answered as he peered over her shoulder. "And I'd like to stay that way, so let's get the hell out of here!"

She needed no further prompting, and they took off running as fast as they could. Five minutes later, they were streaking up the stairs to the bookstore, falling through the door and closing it firmly behind them.

Irene's lungs hurt as she tried to suck in enough air. She locked the front door and raced around the store, pulling down the blinds in every window. "Do you think it will follow us?" she gasped. "Are we safe here?"

The professor had sunk to his knees, his breathing labored. "I- don't- know," he wheezed.

Irene leaned over, placing her hands on her knees as she tried to catch her breath. Muffled footsteps came from the direction of the stairs and a moment later, Benjamin appeared at the landing. It took only a moment for him to assess the situation, and in the next, Irene was cradled in his arms as he gripped her close to him for a moment before he pulled away, his eyes sweeping frantically over her body as his fingers ran over her arms, her shoulders, her hair before gripping her face. His eyes were wild. "You're bleeding!" He reached down and in one sweeping movement, tore a piece of his t-shirt off and began dabbing at her forehead.

Irene's stomach clenched, as much from his impassioned response as from her labored attempts to breath normally. His closeness suddenly seemed right, as if she'd just come home, and she threw her arms around him.

"Oh, Benji," she gasped, tears running down her cheeks in relief. "I'm okay, really. But it was just awful. A wolf. A werewolf. Huge. Just huge!" she shuddered as she remembered.

He clutched her to him. "Darling," he whispered fiercely in her ear. "My sweet girl, I can't take it anymore. I don't care what happens to me, I can't let you go out anymore and risk yourself for me. I couldn't take it if you were hurt." He pulled back and fixed his gaze on hers, stroking her cheek gently. His eyes shimmered and Irene's breath caught in her throat as he shuddered slightly. "You could have been killed tonight and I would have been utterly destroyed."

"Oh, Benji," she whispered, her lips parting, and she surged toward him in the exact same moment he surged toward her.

Their lips met like soldiers on a battlefield, tongues clashing, mouths ravaging each other. He pulled her tightly against him as she snaked her arms around his neck, one hand tangling in his hair.

Benjamin let one hand drop so he could grip her thigh, pulling it up around his waist. Irene moaned.

"Ahem," came an amused voice and they leapt apart.

Both stood staring at Professor McGurty, chests heaving. Irene blushed wildly, realizing she'd forgotten all about the old man.

"I think I'll head upstairs and take a shower," he told them with a small, but knowing smile. "Give you two kids some time to … talk."

Irene watched as he climbed the stairs, and after he

disappeared from sight, she turned back to Benjamin.

His face flamed a fiery red, and she was pretty sure it matched hers. However, regardless of his embarrassment, his eyes still flamed with passion as he stalked forward to take her in his arms again.

"I cannot fight you any longer," he told her, his voice raspy with desire. "And I cannot let you continue searching for answers to my past."

Irene felt herself melting against him, touched that he would give up his chance to crossover for her. "I can't let you do that," she argued with a hush. "I can't let you sacrifice the next thousand years for me."

He barked a harsh laugh. "If I went into eternity with the knowledge that I let harm come to the woman I love, it would be a torturous hell."

Irene inhaled sharply. "Wh-what?" she stammered.

His eyes filled with emotion as he stared down at her, the tension in his jaw relaxing. "I love you, Irene. How could I not? You are kind and generous, so smart and capable, and the most beautiful woman I have ever laid eyes upon." He reached out trembling fingers and traced her collarbone. "And this connection between us is just too much to fight. I no longer want to. I don't want to waste the time I have left with you seeking answers I may never find."

She wrapped herself around him, arms, legs, anything she could do to pull him closer to her. "Are you sure?"

His lips brushed against her ear, sending a shiver down her spine. "Yes, my love.

"Benji," she sighed. "I love you too."

He groaned, capturing her lips with his, his hands lacing through Irene's hair, curling into fist so he could pull her closer. She mimicked him as his tongue ran over the soft underside of her bottom lip.

Moaning, she let her head fall back and his lips blazed a trail down her throat and back up again. His tongue darted into her mouth and she scraped the tip of it with her teeth.

"Irene," he groaned, her name a sweet supplication. "You will drive me mad."

"Benji, please," she begged, her voice dropping so low he could barely hear her. "I want to be alone with you."

He froze for a split second before lifting her chin to look her in the eye. "Are you certain?"

"Please," she whispered.

He heaved a shuddering sigh and scooped her into his arms, carrying her up the stairs, through the living room and into her bedroom, kicking the door shut behind him.

So bold, she realized, suddenly shy and shocked at how she had thrown herself at him. He came from a very different time. Would he think less of her now?

Benjamin sat down next to her. His eyes softened as he took in her fearful expression, and he cupped her cheek in his hand. "If I am to be separated from you in four days, I do not want to waste a single precious moment worrying about what was or what might be. I want only to live in this moment with you," he murmured.

His words melted away her fear and she reached for him. "Hold me," she asked him.

He complied, his body shaking as he gathered her into his arms. She reached up with hesitant lips, kissing him gently. She let the tip of her tongue graze his bottom lip and he groaned.

His obvious pleasure emboldened her, and she ran her hands down the length of his arms, across his chest and over the hard, flat planes of his stomach. She left a trail of light kisses across his cheek, along the outer edge of his ear, and down his neck.

"My sweet girl," he shuddered. "You will unman me."

His hands swept up along the curve of her abdomen, one thumb caressing her belly as it moved up. Further and further, until he brushed along the swell of her breast. She gasped at the contact.

He hesitated and she found the absence of his caress intolerable. She pressed against his hand, encouraging him with a whisper. "Benji," she pleaded. "Please."

He inhaled, his nostrils flaring as he struggled to contain his ardor. His hand moved slowly until it fully cupped her breast, his thumb gently grazed her nipple.

She gasped at the contact, the sharp stinging pleasure it sent shooting through her body, straight down to her core. She felt her nipple pucker, under his ministrations, straining for his touch.

How did I not know? She thought wildly. *How did I never understand what it could be like between a man and a woman?*

Her back arched, her body surging toward him, and he hesitated for moment.

"Irene?" he whispered. "I ache for you."

Desire flared inside her. "I ache for you as well. Please, Benji. I need to be closer to you."

He trembled as he ran a hand along the hem of her blouse before slipping it underneath so he could caress her belly. His fingers blazed a trail higher, pulling her blouse up inch by inch to reveal the creamy skin of her stomach. Leaning over, he kissed her bellybutton.

Gasping, she arched against him. He made a sound of pleasure in the back of his throat and began to unbutton her blouse. He held the last one in his fingers for a moment before pushing the fabric back over her shoulders.

"Oh, Irene," he sighed as his eyes feasted on the lacy white bra pulled taut across her alabaster mounds. He traced the outline of her breast with a forefinger. "You are exquisite."

He let his finger trace the edge of her bra before slipping beneath the fabric to graze the flesh of her nipple.

"Oh!" Pleasure coursed through her, but a moment later it exploded inside her as he pulled the fabric down, releasing her breast, then leaning down to take her nipple in his mouth. She grasped his head. "Benjamin!" she panted as his tongue flicked her nipple. "Oh, Benji!"

He reached up to pull her bra down, releasing her second breast and kneading it with one hand. She closed her eyes, writhing beneath his touch.

She cried out a moment later when his hands disappeared. Opening her eyes, however, she inhaled sharply as she realized he was removing his shirt. Staring down at her, he fingered her bra. "How do we take this off?"

Irene sat up, reaching behind her to unclasp her bra. As it fell away, Benjamin gasped. "Oh, sweet girl, you are beautiful."

"I want to see all of you," he told her, asking her permission with his eyes.

She nodded. "Only if I can see all of you," she answered.

He shook with restrained passion as he pulled her

jeans down the silky length of her legs, leaning down to place gentle kisses on the tender inner flesh of her thighs. She cried out. When she finally lay naked under his gaze, he pulled his own jeans off before gathering her against him. His hot flesh burned against hers.

"You feel so good," she whispered dreamily.

"As do you," he responded as his body covered hers. She felt his manhood surge against her thigh and she gyrated with need against him.

Groaning, he reached down and stilled her. "Please, my love, be still, else I lose control."

Knowing he wanted her so much, his words emboldened her and she moved against him again.

"Vixen," he gritted before yanking her against him. His mouth plundered hers and before long, she was gasping for breath as her head swam.

He moved lower, his mouth plundering her body as he had her mouth, and she cried out softly as her body rose up off the bed toward him. He left a wet trail down her belly until he hovered over her core.

He hesitated for a moment, until she thought she might explode. "Benji," she begged, and it seemed to be what he had been waiting for.

His tongue dipped into her tender flesh, finding the sweet jewel of her womanhood.

Her head fell back as sensations rocked her body. Never had she felt such pleasure. His thumb followed his tongue, stroking the entrance of her core and her breath came in mewling gasps.

"Please," she panted. "Oh, please." She had no idea what she was asking for, she only knew she'd never experienced anything like his touch in her entire life and she wanted more.

Then he pushed a finger inside her while his tongue continued to tease her sensitive nub. Her body arched off the bed as she exploded around him. "Benji," she cried incoherently.

His mouth left her flesh and he pressed his body against hers again, his hot flesh resting against her opening. She strained toward him.

"Are you certain?" he asked her, his voice hoarse with need. "I need you to tell me you are sure."

"Yes, my love," she gasped. "I am sure."

A moment later, she felt him enter her, his hard shaft filling her up. He sank into her, fully sheathing himself in her warm depths. Irene felt a slight twinge of pain and winced slightly. He froze.

A moment later, he seemed to understand. "Oh, my girl," he pulled back to stare down at her with wide eyes. "You've never ... how? What about the sex, drugs and rock and roll?"

She smiled, holding back a laugh before reaching up to stroke his cheek. "I never wanted to before," she whispered tenderly. "Please, Benjamin, don't stop."

He shuddered almost violently and pulled back, almost completely unsheathing himself before sinking back into her again.

This time there was no pain. Tension began to build in her, low in the pit of her belly as he thrust inside her over and over, filling her, stretching her flesh delightfully.

His breathing became labored and his thrusts took on an urgency. Irene wrapped her legs around his waist, lifting her hips to meet him. The pressure in her belly grew to almost unbearable heights. He seemed to feel it too as his body seemed to tremble with barely contained energy.

"My love," he cried out, thrusting hard inside her.

It was enough to send her over the edge. The tension inside her exploded, blocking out all sensation except that of the man above her, inside her, and the incredible waves of pleasure that rocked her body.

A moment later, he seemed to convulse inside her, his body growing taut, and he cried out again. "Irene!"

His body jerked once, twice, and then he collapsed on her, resting his weight on his elbows. He kissed her neck, her cheek, her lips, shuddering with his release.

They stayed that way for several seconds, then he gathered her in his arms and turned them both over so she could lay across his chest.

"I love you, sweet girl," he murmured as she relaxed against him.

"Oh, Benji, I love you too," she whispered as contentment washed over her, pulling her down into the comforting arms of sleep.

CHAPTER SIXTEEN

Day Four

I rene woke much later to find herself still laying on top of Benji. She could tell by his breathing that he was asleep, although his strong arms were still wrapped around her.

She smiled against his chest.

You are a wild woman, she told herself with delicious satisfaction. *You're one of those women in Benji's books.*

Ah, inserted Holmes. *I see you've finally succumbed to your nature.*

The last word was laced with condescension, and Irene frowned. *So?* She challenged. *I let you convince me all these years that human relationships were too messy, too inconvenient to be worthwhile. I let you keep me isolated all these years!*

My dear, I have done nothing to you. I have merely shared my point of view. That it is dispassionate is not a disappointment to me. It is who I am.

What do you know? She countered angrily. *After all, you're not even a real person. You're just a fictional character. A one-dimensional character at that!*

Indeed, he mocked. *Then pray tell, my dear Miss Bell, why have you listened to me all these years?*

She was opening her mouth to respond before he finished speaking, but found herself speechless instead. He was right. Why *had* she listened to him all these years?

She'd always thought of him as the prudent, logical side of her psyche, the one leading her down a path of safety and security.

Now she realized he was the voice of all her fears and insecurity. He had never kept her safe, he'd only kept her down. Hidden and alone.

My dear Holmes, she responded archly. *I believe it is time to retire our acquaintance. I don't think I wish to talk with you anymore.*

Ah, he responded ruefully. *This is, perhaps, a moment that has been a long time coming. I imagine you will be the better for it. One does, after all, have to trust their own instincts about any other. If you are finally ready to trust your own rather than mine, then you no longer have a need for me.*

No, I don't believe that I do.

Very good, he responded, tipping his hat most formally. *I bid you a fond farewell, my dear Miss Bell.*

"Goodbye," she whispered.

Benjamin's hands moved, one hand sweeping down

her back to rest on the back of her thigh, the other settling against her head as his fingers laced through her hair. "Who are you talking to?" he murmured, still half asleep.

"No one," she answered. "Just to myself."

He kissed the top of her head, letting his hands wander across her body.

"Mmm," she arched against him.

He groaned and she felt his body stirring against her thigh. "We must see to the professor," he sighed.

The professor! Irene froze for a moment before leaping out of bed. "Oh my goodness." She raced about the room in a panic, pulling her clothes on. "I didn't make him dinner, and he's probably starving for breakfast." She glanced at her clock. "Eight-twenty! I have to open the store at nine. How could I have been so thoughtless?"

"I'm hungry too," Benjamin offered. "Do you have more bacon in that wonderful icebox of yours?" She threw his pants at him, and he snickered as they hit him in the face.

"Get dressed," she ordered as she tried to straighten her hair.

He stood, pulling his pants on. "Irene, calm down. The professor is an intelligent man, as well as understanding. He will not fault you."

He moved to stand in front of her, pulling her into his arms. "He understands that we only have a few, short days together."

She paused, looking up at him. The warmth in his eyes pierced through her panic and she rested against him. "You're right. I will have all the time I want to talk to him when you're gone." A lump formed in her throat at the thought.

He squeezed her tightly for a moment and then she stepped away, holding her hand out for his. He took it willingly. "Come, let's have breakfast." She smiled up at him.

Professor McGurty was already in the kitchen. Coffee had been brewed and he sat reading quietly. He looked up with a smile when they entered. "Good morning," he greeted. "I trust you both slept well?"

He gave no indication of meaning anything but genuine concern and Irene relaxed, smiling back at him. "Yes, I did. Are you hungry?"

He nodded, rubbing his flat belly. "Famished, my dear."

"Well, we better make this quick, then," she laughed. "I have to open the store in half an hour."

Day Five / Day Six

Irene turned the sign in her store window from closed to open with seconds to spare. Professor McGurty had begged off their company two days prior, telling them he needed to go home for a day or two. "Things have settled, and don't worry," he held up a hand to ward them off. "I'll call you if I need anything."

Since then, she and Benjamin had spent every spare second in each other's arms, learning all they could about each other. Now, after two days alone together, they were still fascinated with each other.

When the door to the store was unlocked, Benjamin pulled her into the classic fiction room where a comfortable old leather couch sat between two bookshelves.

The sat talking for more than two hours, telling each other about their childhoods, school, and anything else that came to mind.

Irene lay with her head in his lap, staring up at him when the bell on the door jangled for the first time all week. She sat up quickly.

A lean, handsome man with messy light-brown locks and sharp cheekbones walked in.

Benjamin's eyebrows shot up. "You were the man who came in with Albert," he said, his eyes narrowing. "You took a book from the store without paying."

Irene placed a restraining hand on his shoulder and stood up. "Can I help you?"

"Name's Liam," he growled, looking irritated as he pulled a wad of cash out of his pocket. "Albert has been hounding me to come back in and pay for the book I took. He said it was stealing." He rolled his eyes. "I told him desperate times call for desperate measures, but here I am, nonetheless. God only knows why."

"Well, I have no idea what book you took or how much it was," she answered kindly. "But I agree, things around town have been rather … unusual lately. I understand."

"Oh hell, no," Liam grimaced. "I can't go back without being able to tell him I paid for the damn book. The tag said $39.95." He plunked down two twenties and a five on the counter as Irene approached. "That should cover tax too."

Benjamin joined her behind the counter as she rang

up the sale, handing him his change and a receipt. "Here's your proof," she grinned at him.

He snorted, and Irene could swear he was trying to hide a smile.

"I'll give this to Albert," he scoffed with a wry smile, holding up the receipt, turning to leave.

"Wait," Benjamin called after him, a strange urgency in his voice.

Irene glanced up at him, puzzled by the queer look on his face. He came around the counter, pointing at Liam's chest. "That's Albert's, isn't it?"

Liam glanced down, before picking up the rather feminine looking gemstone charm hanging on a chain around his neck. "This? Yes, it was Albert's. He gave it to me. For … safe keeping."

Benjamin's eyes narrowed. "I can't believe it," he muttered to himself. "How did I not see it before? It's the gemstone."

Irene realized what he was talking about and looked at it with new interest. "You don't mean …" she breathed.

He nodded. "Yes, I do. It's the stone from the Star Anthame."

Liam took a step back, looking at them suspiciously. "What the hell do you know about the Anthame?" he demanded.

Benjamin's nostrils flared with irritation. "I could ask you the same question, sir," he countered.

The two men seemed to square off for a moment until it became obvious to Irene that neither of them would back down first.

"Oh, for goodness sake," she moved between them. She turned to Liam first. "Look, Benjamin was killed with the Anthame, cursing him to remain in limbo. If we want to break the curse, we need to fully assemble the Anthame, and that," she pointed at the gem, "Is the only piece we have left to find."

She turned and stared at Benjamin pointedly. "And is that anyway to behave toward someone who has something we need?"

Benjamin held up a hand. "Wait, wait, wait. We already decided we were done with this. I told you I wasn't willing to risk your safety again."

"But you're not," she argued. "I didn't have to go looking for it at all. It came to us. We know about the remaining pieces. Everything is falling in place like it's meant to be ..." She recalled Flora's words from their last visit.

Everything will work out exactly as it is meant to.

"Benjamin," she gripped his arm. "I know you said you weren't willing to risk me, but there's no risk here. And how could we live with ourselves if we let the witch continue hurting people? There is more at stake here than just us."

Benjamin studied her for a moment, his jaw clenching before he nodded slightly.

"Hold up," Liam snapped, and they turned to look at him. "What makes you think I'm going to give you the gem in the first place?"

"Because we have the other pieces," Irene snapped back. "And the only thing standing between us stopping an evil bitch of a witch is that gem." She pointed at it, glaring at him.

He stared back at her, lifting his hands a moment later to remove the chain from his neck. "Whoa, there, little lady, no need to get so fired up."

Irene continued to glare at him as he dropped the gem in her outstretched hand. "Thank you," she said tersely.

He nodded, his expression turning serious for the first time since he'd come in the store. "Take care of the witch, but please return the stone when you're finished."

Irene felt her irritation melt away as she closed her fist around the gem. "I will make sure it finds its way back to you."

He gave her one last curt nod before he left, the door closing behind him with a slam and a jangle.

Benjamin and Irene stared at each other for a moment before they both spoke at once.

"I can't believe it."

"Never in a million years would I have guessed the stone would just walk into my store."

They grinned at each other, and Irene picked up the receiver to the store phone. "We have to call the professor," she told him.

His face lit up. "Let me," he asked eagerly.

She smothered a laugh. She'd been showing him how to use various technology over the last couple days. He'd relished in learning how to use all of it, grasping the concepts with the ease and delight of a child.

Slowly he pushed the buttons on the cordless phone, dialing the professor's number. He'd called the older man multiple times over the last couple days. When the professor answered, Benjamin's face broke out in a grin. "Professor," he spoke slowly, enunciating each syllable, almost yelling. "Can you hear me?"

He paused. "We have news. We found the last piece of the Anthame." A moment later, he turned to Irene. "Am

I yelling?"

She broke out in gales of laughter, and nodded. "Oh, yes, you most certainly are."

The professor arrived at the store a short time later and they sat around a table in the contemporary fiction room discussing the new discovery as they tried to formulate a plan to defeat the witch.

"If she's still in love with this Isaac Parker, our path seems clear," reasoned Professor McGurty. "We have to enlist his help. Flora was clear that he would be the only way to get to Priscilla."

"Edith," came a voice behind them.

They whirled to find Isaac Parker leaning against the doorway as Anika rolled her eyes slightly.

"What?" asked the professor.

"The witch. Her name is Edith. Or at least it was when I knew her," he finished.

"Wait," Irene stood, walking over to peer at the door. "How did you get in without the bell jangling?"

"Very carefully," Isaac quipped. "But that's not why we're here. We realized we need you to give us the blade. We have to stop the witch. Killing her is the only way to stop her, and I don't trust anyone else to do it."

Benjamin gave him an appraising look as Irene came back to stand by his side. "Even if we give you the blade, you still need the gemstone."

Isaac raised an eyebrow. "Would you happen to be

the ghost Irene told us about?" he asked.

"Perhaps." He put a protective arm around Irene.

"The witch Flora has already broken the curse on me. But I still need to make sure she doesn't do to anyone else what she did to me. Or you," he said pointedly. "I'd think you'd want to help."

"I want her wiped out of existence," Benjamin growled. "That doesn't mean I have any reason to trust you."

"Benjamin," Irene admonished softly, placing a hand on his chest and looking up at him. "We can trust them. Even Flora said we would have to work together."

He looked down at her, his arm tightening around her for a moment before he looked at Isaac again. "You're going to take her out yourself?"

A fierce look crossed Isaac's face. "Nothing would give me more pleasure," he snarled with savage delight.

"I don't want Irene anywhere near you when the time comes," Benjamin added.

"Good, because neither do I," Isaac retorted. "That's why you need to give us the blade now."

"Wait," Irene piped up. "We still need the Anthame to break the curse on Benjamin."

Benjamin let out an exasperated sigh. "We discussed this already. Nothing is more important than getting rid of the witch."

"You're wrong," she insisted. "Even if Isaac is successful and kills Priscilla-"

"Edith," Isaac interrupted.

Irene flashed him a dirty look. "Whatever. Even if he kills her, the Star Anthame is still in existence. What if someone else finds it and uses it like she did? We know how to break its power. We have to end it, once and for all."

"That's right," Anika stepped forward. "You told us that when we ran into you the other day. There's a prophecy, right?"

Irene nodded. "Yes. And between us and the two of you, we have all the pieces of the Anthame."

A cacophony of voices exploded throughout the room.

"Irene!" Benjamin protested.

"What the hell?" Isaac growled.

"Seriously?" Anika asked excitedly. "You have the gem?"

"The plot thickens!" Professor McGurty laughed.

"Oh. My. God." Irene rolled her eyes. "Would everyone just shut the hell up!"

Silence filled the room. Everyone stood looking at her in gaped-mouth surprise, none more so than Benjamin.

"Look," she snapped at no one in particular. "Here's what's going to happen. Tomorrow night, you and you," she pointed first to Anika, then Isaac, "Are going to figure out how to get the witch here-"

Anika held up a hand. "Ah, ah, ah! Already taken care of!" She grinned when Irene gave her a startled look. "She'll be here tomorrow night."

Irene's eyes narrowed. "How did you know I'd help you? And further, how did you know we'd have the other two pieces of the Anthame?"

Anika's eyes danced with a shrewd humor as she shrugged. "I kind of figured you'd need our help as much as we needed yours and neither of us had much of a choice. And I had no idea you'd have the other pieces."

Her grin widened. "But I hoped."

"Fine," Irene said crossly, cocking a hip and slapping a hand on it. "Good. Come early. When you get here, we'll assemble the Anthame together."

Isaac and Benjamin both opened their mouths to speak and she glared at each of them. "It's better that one person doesn't have all the pieces until the last possible moment.

"After we assemble the relic, you'll take care of the witch, give me back the Anthame, and you can be on your way."

She glared at each person in the room one by one. "Anyone got anything to say?" she challenged, hands on her hips. A low mumbling round of no's went round the room. "That's what I thought," she snapped.

"Well, uh, I guess we'll see you tomorrow," Isaac muttered, rubbing the back of his neck awkwardly.

"Yes," she gritted. "Let me know when we should expect you."

She walked them out, Anika pausing at the door. "That was awesome," she whispered with wicked delight in Irene's ear. "When this is all said and done, we're going to have to invest in some quality girl time." A mischievous grin crossed her face as the door closed behind her.

Irene suppressed a grin as she watched the other woman walk away. Somehow, in the two short meetings she'd had with Anika, she'd grown to like her. *I think I'm going to like this girl time thing,* she thought as she locked the door and pulled the blinds.

"Can I have a moment of your time?" Benjamin asked Professor McGurty.

The professor glanced at Irene for a moment. "Absolutely. However," he made a show of yawning and stretching. "I think I'd like to turn in early tonight. And in my own bed too. As long as I skedaddle before dark, I think I'll be safe."

"I don't think anyone is safe until the rift closes," Irene retorted.

"True," he agreed. "So let's say I'm as safe as I'll ever be. At least I won't have to deal with werewolves!"

Benjamin glanced at Irene. "Would you give the good professor and I a few minutes? I have some things I'd like to discuss with him."

Irene rolled her eyes. "I hope it's not some macho crap like 'watch over her when I'm gone' or something like that," she snapped at him, immediately regretting it. She knew it was exactly like that and even though she didn't care a lick if he asked the professor to look after her, she was having a hard time fighting her own emotions.

"Macho?" Benjamin asked, his brow wrinkling with confusion.

"Oh, never mind," she answered crossly. "I'll be in the kitchen where I belong. Making dinner."

She stormed away, berating herself the entire time. Why, oh why couldn't she just tell him how scared she was? How she wasn't sure how to deal with the fact that in a few short hours, he would be gone?

She moved around the kitchen, pulling pots out of cupboards, slamming the doors shut, and generally making a racket. As she began to slice up some vegetables for steaming, she felt two strong hands rest lightly on her shoulders. She froze at the touch.

"Irene," Benjamin murmured. "You do not need to act as if you are my mother. I am not a macho man who expects you to cook my meals, polish my boots or wipe my face."

She smiled despite herself. Clearly the professor had explained the term "macho" to him in his usual eccentric fashion.

"If I let you use the stove, you'd probably burn the house down," she muttered, turning to look at him.

"That seems a bit of an exaggeration." Benjamin gave her the wounded look of an errant child after a scolding. "I concede I might burn the food, but certainly not the entire house."

She laughed at his expression and how much it reminded her of when she caught him reading romance novels. Even with his intelligence and overt masculinity, he still managed to possess a childlike quality. A freshness, an innocence, she realized, and it reminded her of the prophecy. Her laugh morphed into a choked sob. "You'd probably burn down the entire square if I wasn't here to stop you," she tried to tease, but her eyes filled with tears and she couldn't stop herself from wrapping her arms around him, gripping him tightly.

His arms snaked around her and he held her just as tightly.

"How am I supposed to let you go?" Irene wept against his chest.

"Shh," he tried to soothe her. "I never should have let things go so far between us. I'm the worst kind of selfish cad. My only excuse is that I loved you the moment I opened my eyes and thought I was looking up at an angel. I just hope that someday after I'm gone, you don't grow to regret what happened between us."

"No!" she protested, looking up at him and shaking

her head fiercely. "That will never happen. I'm not sorry about any of it, but if I have to lose you no matter what, I'd like to do it knowing I did the right thing."

"I was a fool to think we could pretend like all of this had just gone away. I just wanted to keep you from all this." His jaw clenched. "I only wanted to keep you safe."

"And I wanted to steal time with you but I knew it was just that: stealing time. I knew it three days ago when Flora told me fate had already decided. I knew we wouldn't be able to avoid any of it." She reached up and cupped his cheek. "We still have one night together."

His gaze softened. "Yes, we do," he uttered hoarsely just before his lips captured hers. A moment later he scooped her up and carried her off to the bedroom.

CHAPTER SEVENTEEN

Day Seven

Morning dawned, bringing a somberness with it. Irene woke to find herself wrapped in Benjamin's arms. She glanced out the window, noticing frost along the edges of the panes for the first time since fall swept over Saint's Grove.

They had spent the previous night making love and whispering into the wee hours of the morning until they could no longer keep their eyes open, neither of them willing to lose a moment together.

Irene shivered from the morning cold and pulled the blankets up around her neck, snuggling closer to Benjamin. He stirred but didn't wake, instead, he pulled her tighter against him.

She went willingly. The day she would lose him had come, and nothing would tear her from his side in these last hours.

How has he managed to change my whole life in such a short time? She wondered. *Such things only happen in books, like those romance novels he loves to read.* She smiled at the thought, deciding that after he was gone, perhaps she would have to read one of his books, just to see if it was worthwhile.

After he was gone.

Her throat seemed to close up and she tried, unsuccessfully, to choke back tears. They slipped down her cheek and onto his bare chest. The day had come and there was no avoiding it.

Benjamin reached up and stroked her hair. "Please do not cry, my sweet girl," he pleaded, his voice low and hoarse with emotion. "I don't think I will be able to hold back my own tears if you do."

She pulled herself up to kiss his lips. "I will miss you more than I have ever missed anyone in my entire life."

He groaned, pulling her up to slant his mouth over hers, his tongue grazing her lips. She responded eagerly, reaching up to run her fingers through his hair.

A moment later, she found herself on her back while his hands ran down the length of her body. She arched against him. "Benji," she sighed.

His mouth followed his hands, nibbling his way down to her soft, feminine core. A moment later she cried out with delight as his tongue found her nub.

"Please, Benji," she pleaded. "I need you."

He moved up, staring down at her for a moment as his already hard arousal proved her center. She lifted her hips, teasing him and he groaned as he slid inside her.

"Sweet girl," he breathed as he pulled back, plunging inside her once more.

Irene pushed against him, and a moment later he gathered her in his arms, sitting up so she straddled him. His lips brushed against hers as his hands moved down to her hips, guiding her movements.

Irene gasped at the sensations the new angle provided. She moved slowly, letting her head fall back as she experienced fresh waves of pleasure.

"Benji," she moaned as his mouth traveled up and down her throat. She held onto his shoulders, her hips gyrating against his, pressure mounting until it spilled over and Irene cried out with her release. Benjamin followed her a moment later, his arms tightening around her as he voiced his own pleasure.

Irene sighed, resting against his chest as he hugged her tightly. She felt herself drifting off again, and he tenderly laid her down in the bed, kissing her temple lightly. "Sleep, my darling girl," he whispered, and she smiled sleepily at him before she closed her eyes again and let herself succumb to sleep.

The shrill cry of the fire alarm woke her sometime later. She sat up, frightened when Benjamin was nowhere to be found and rushed from the bedroom in a panic.

The apartment was filled with smoke, but she couldn't stop the grin that spread across her face when she heard cursing coming from the kitchen.

"Bloody hell! Blasted contraption! Damn infernal machine!"

She peeked through the doorway to find Benjamin standing over the stove with a pan full of burned bacon, looking wildly about for the source of the noise.

"Can I help you?" she called over the alarm, smothering a laugh.

He whirled and stared at her. A moment later he threw his hands up in the air. "I wanted to prove to you I would not burn the house down."

She couldn't hold back her laugh anymore, and giggled madly as she moved to pull the charred mess of the stove. "Help me open the windows to air out the house," she grinned at him as she grabbed a towel and began fanning the fire alarm in the living room. A few moments later, the alarm ceased and Benjamin let out a sigh of relief.

"I am sorry," he told her, shame-faced. "I've watched you use that machine, it seemed simple enough."

She reached up to kiss him. "Why don't you let me take care of breakfast while you call Professor McGurty and find out what time he'll be coming over?"

He brightened, nodding in agreement and she could only shake her head in amusement as she returned to the kitchen to start breakfast. Again.

The day progressed too quickly for Irene's liking. By the time the professor arrived, the afternoon had given way to early evening, bringing a maudlin quality with it.

The three of them sat around a table in the store, talking quietly about nonsense subjects and trying to avoid what they all knew was coming. Benjamin kept the blade in his pocket and Irene had put the gemstone around her neck. She spent most of the time fingering it nervously.

Finally night fell and a nervous energy thrummed through all of them. Benjamin began pacing the room as they waited for Anika and Isaac to arrive.

"Everything will be all right, son," the professor tried to assure him.

Benjamin glanced at Irene. "I sincerely hope you are right, sir."

"Mycroft," the professor told him lightly. He smiled when Benjamin looked puzzled. "It's my name. We're all friends here, and I prefer my friends call me Mycroft."

"Mycroft," Benjamin echoed, then smiled. "Very well, Mycroft. I sincerely hope you are right." The door jangled at that moment and he jumped.

They turned to watch Anika and Isaac walk through the door.

They all looked at each other for a moment, then Isaac walked over to the table and placed something on it.

It was the hilt of the Star Anthame.

Irene went next, taking the chain holding the gemstone from around her neck and placing it next to the hilt. Benjamin followed suit, placing the blade on the table as well. The small group stood staring at them for a moment.

"A rather unassuming assembly of artifacts, don't you think?" quipped the professor.

Irene leaned against Benjamin. "They certainly don't look like they have any special power."

"Let's get this thing put together," Isaac said, moving to do just that.

It took a few minutes to fit the pieces in place, but once aligned correctly, they seemed to snap together.

Anika raised an eyebrow. "Well, that seemed simple

enough."

"Yes," Isaac agreed. "But the next task won't be." He glanced at Benjamin, then Irene. "We better get outside."

They walked toward the door, and Irene followed.

"Irene," Benjamin tried to stop her.

She gave him a pointed look. "I'll be back. I promise."

Irene stood with Anika on the porch of the bookstore, watching Isaac pace beneath the street lamp. She wrapped her arms around herself and shivered. "It's cold tonight," she remarked, glancing up and down the street, wondering when the witch would arrive.

Anika nodded in agreement. "The coldest it's been all year. Do you think it has anything to do with what's coming?"

"Most likely," Irene said. "Are you afraid?" she added suddenly, turning to look Anika in the eye. "I am."

Sighing, Anika closed her fist around the dagger. "Terrified … but, I have to see this through for Isaac."

Irene smiled at the other woman. "You love him, don't you?"

Anika gazed back out into the night at Isaac, who had stopped pacing and now stood leaning against the wrought iron light fixture. He glanced up to meet Anika's gaze and smiled. "I do," she confessed. "It seems insane to me to love someone so much when you've only known him for a week. But, I guess that's not really the whole story. I mean … I've always known him, I just didn't realize it."

Irene choked back a laugh. "At least you've got the whole reincarnation thing going for you. I've literally only known Benji for six days, but …" She trailed off, but Anika nodded and she knew the other woman understood her perfectly.

Anika opened her mouth to answer when a shadow appeared in the square, angling toward them across the patch of green grass. Anika straightened, watching as she came closer and Isaac turned to face her.

"It's her," Irene said, her voice low and breathless.

"Go inside," Anika commanded. "Don't come out for any reason. When we're done, I'll bring the dagger back inside and hand it to you."

Irene scurried back inside, a wild expression on her face when she looked at the professor and Benjamin. "She's here," she whispered. "Priscilla is here."

All three of them rushed to the window and watched with bated breath.

The figure approached the store until the street lights illuminated her face.

"Lisa," whispered the professor.

"Shh," Irene hushed him as she watched the scene unfold.

"You're late," Isaac accused the witch.

She flashed him a sly smile. "Were you anxious for my company, Isaac? I had no idea you'd missed me so much."

His entire body tensed. His jaw ticked and Anika placed a hand on his arm until he took a deep breath. "Let's get this over with. We have the relic here, as promised."

"I want to see it," Priscilla/Edith demanded.

Anika revealed the blade, raising it to the moonlight but remaining careful not to put it within the other woman's reach. "It's here. But there's still the matter we discussed before, Edith."

The witch rolled her eyes. "You mean my promise you leave the two of you alone forever in eternal bliss?"

"I want your word," Isaac demanded. "It's the payment I require in exchange for the Star Anthame. You get the relic, me and Anika get to live in peace without you dogging our every step. Agree to the terms, or there's no deal."

Even from a distance it was clear she only pretended to consider his demand. "Hmm," she mused mockingly. "I suppose I could be convinced to agree to those terms … with one added condition."

"What now?" Isaac spat.

"A kiss," she replied, flashing a smug grin at Anika.

Anika stiffened before giving Isaac a curt nod. "Do it. This is our only chance."

Edith/Priscilla laughed, the sound sending chills down Irene's back. "That's right, lovers. Your only chance at happiness together lies with me. Isaac, I suggest you do your best … we both know what the consequences are for disappointing me."

Irene was certain he was going to argue for a moment, but then he stepped forward, closing the distance between them.

"I can't see," Benjamin ground out in frustration as Isaac stepped between them and the witch.

They could hear her, however. "Like you mean it, Isaac. Or I'll tear your woman to shreds and make you watch."

"Bitch," snarled Benjamin, shocking Irene with his vehemence. His expression softened when he looked at her. "I would kill her for threatening you like that."

They watched in horror as Isaac's head lowered and

the Edith/Priscilla's arms wrapped around him. The kiss went on for several long, uncomfortable moments. Irene wanted to look away but found she couldn't.

Suddenly, Edith/Priscilla's legs gave out from under her and she sunk to the ground. Isaac followed her, finally tearing his mouth from hers and straddling her as he pressed her against the concrete with a hand at her throat.

"B-belladonna!" She tried to fight him off, but to no avail. "You … son of a … bitch!"

He grinned with savage triumph, easily keeping her pinned now that the herb had sapped her strength. "You did ask me for a kiss, Edith. So sorry I forgot to mention the belladonna capsule under my tongue."

Anika rushed to his side, handing him the blade. "Finish it," she told him.

"Gladly," he snarled, raising the dagger high in the air.

A new voice broke through the darkness of the night. "No, don't!"

Irene, Benjamin and the professor gasped in unison as they watched a man come hurtling out of the darkness. He tackled Isaac, knocking him off the witch as a second man followed close behind and watched from a safe distance.

Irene recognized the first man as Mark, Lisa's brother.

Anika stepped forward. "No! Stop!"

"Let go!" Isaac bellowed, fighting to free himself from the other man. "You have to let me go. She has to die!"

"You're not laying a hand on my sister!" Mark continued to fight Isaac.

Rushing toward them, Anika pried the Star Anthame

from Isaac's grip. "That isn't your sister," she told him. "That is a witch, possessing your sister, and this is the only way to free her."

Mark's companion frowned, gazing at the dagger she clutched in her fist. "Is that what I think it is?"

Anika nodded. "The Star Anthame, yes. You have to let us stab her with it. It won't kill Lisa, but it'll purge her of the witch. She'll never be the same if we don't do something, and fast!"

Mark glanced up at the other man who gave him a nod, his mouth a grim line. "She's right."

Glancing back and forth from her to this man he seemed to trust, Mark clenched his jaw. "If she dies …"

"She won't," Isaac snarled. "But I will if you don't get the hell out of our way."

Mark let him go, and Isaac struggled to his feet as Anika turned back toward the spot where the witch had been, only to find it empty.

"There she is!" Irene squealed, pointing as Edith/Priscilla lunged toward Isaac, but it was too late. The witch held a dagger of her own, and she gleefully plunged it into Isaac's stomach.

Irene let out a tiny scream as the woman pulled the dagger out and thrust it into his gut again.

A terrible expression crossed Anika's face and she rushed the witch from behind. She wrapped her arm around Edith/Priscilla's neck yanking her back before she could pull the knife free again. Anika raised her free arm, still holding the Star Anthame and drove it straight into the witch's chest.

Edith/Priscilla screamed and fell to her knees. Some unseen force shoved Anika away from her, knocking her to the ground next to Isaac.

The witch thrashed wildly as her body convulsed.

Mark tried to go to her, but his companion held him back, shaking his head. Anika crawled toward Isaac as a dark shadow peeled itself away from Lisa's body.

"Edith's true form," Isaac declared.

The shadow poured from her like fog, rising high in the air. Her screams finally faded as Lisa's body finally seemed to relax, still breathing but still.

Mark finally ran to his sister, dropping to his knees. He slipped a hand under her head, hugging her tightly to him before turning to Isaac and Anika. "Thank you," he told them as he wiped away his tears.

Irene watched the scene, wiping away her own tears.

Isaac, however, was clearly hurting. "You're welcome," he managed as he worked to inhale and exhale.

Mark glanced down at Isaac's wound. "Sorry I got you stabbed."

Isaac barked a laugh. "Don't worry about it. I wanted to die anyway."

Mark looked puzzled.

Anika picked up the Star Anthame. "Wait here," Anika she told Isaac, glancing at the bookstore.

Irene met her at the door, gesturing at Isaac with a frown. "Is he going to be okay?"

"Not if I don't get him back on his side of the rift," Anika replied. Without waiting for a response, she hurried back to Isaac as Mark and his friend helped Lisa across the square.

Benjamin and the professor joined Irene on the porch as they watched Anika help Isaac off the ground and toward the statue of Peter Saint. "Come on, old man," they heard her quip. "Let's get you home."

CHAPTER EIGHTEEN

I rene, Benjamin and Professor McGurty stared at one another, still stunned by what they had witnessed.

"That was … something," Irene finished lamely.

"Indeed," the professor agreed.

Benjamin nodded with a frown. "Now what?" he asked.

Irene fought back tears. She knew what came next. They all did. She felt her fingers tighten around the relic in her hand and looked down at it, feeling a sudden hatred for the artifact. Never in her life had she hated an inanimate object, but she did now.

The professor laid a hand on Benjamin's shoulder. "It has been a privilege knowing you," he told the young man, his eyes shimmering. "I wish it could have been a much longer friendship."

Benjamin seemed to almost choke, a hand coming up to grip his hair for a moment before he reached out and hugged the old man to him. "The feeling is mutual, my friend," he answered in a garbled voice. "Please take care of her."

They let go of each other a few moments later and Benjamin turned to Irene.

She stared up at him, or at least tried to, but her eyes filled with tears until her vision blurred. She dashed them away angrily.

"Irene," he managed.

"Benjamin," she mouthed, unable to make a sound.

He had just stepped toward her when a terrible snarl filled the air around them.

A moment later, a huge gray object barreled across the porch toward Irene, knocking the Anthame from her grasp and backward over the railing.

"Werewolf!" she heard the professor shout.

The same one from before, she realized, her hands pushing against its neck as she fought to avoid its snapping teeth. She could see a cross-shaped scar on the roof of its mouth. Saliva dripped from its mouth into her hair.

"Irene!" she heard Benjamin's panicked cry.

A split second later, she heard Professor McGurty yell, "Benjamin! No," as the weight of the wolf left her body and it howled in pain.

She rolled over, horrified to see that Benjamin had leapt from the porch to knock the wolf off her and plunge the Star Anthame into its chest.

Benjamin sank to his knees as he began to fade.

"Dear God," Professor McGurty cried. "Irene! What do we do?"

"Get back on the porch," she called to him, tears streaking down her face. "Please, Benji, get back on the porch!"

He crawled toward the porch as his strength left him, inching closer and closer until his hands finally grasped the bottom step. His fingers seemed to solidify for a moment, then fade, then solidify again. Back and forth they went as the rest of his body faded away until Irene could see the grass beneath him.

"Grab his hands," she shrieked at the professor. "Grab them while they're solid!"

He complied, dragging what was left of Benjamin back on the porch.

Irene rushed to his side, watching anxiously for his form to coalesce again, breathing a sigh of relief when it finally did.

Behind them, the wolf continued to shriek. Benjamin was still too weak to move, but Irene was able to lift him up enough to see what was happening.

All three of them watched as the wolf convulsed, his body shrinking and morphing the entire time. Its fur seemed to bubble and change, shriveling away until finally all that remained was the bared, naked flesh of a man. The Star Anthame fell to the ground next to him as blood dripped from his chest.

He rested on his hands and knees, panting with great effort. Finally he looked up. He seemed oddly familiar to Irene, but she knew that she didn't know him.

One of their little group did, however.

"Dear God," Benjamin gasped. "Armin?"

Irene's eyes widened as she studied the man closer. She saw now that the familiarity she'd recognized in him was the similarities in his features to Benjamin. He was handsome like Benjamin, but his eyes lacked the intelligence of his brother. He looked as though he'd been through hell. His hair was wild, streaked with gray, and his face had been weathered and lined.

She held Benjamin tightly in her arms. "You're saying he's your brother?" she whispered.

He struggled to sit up, intent on the other man who looked up at him, tears streaming down his face. "Armin, how did you get here?"

"I'm sorry, brother," Armin sobbed. "I couldn't help it."

Benjamin started to pull himself across the porch, still too weak to stand, but Irene put her hand in his shoulder. "You can't," she reminded him with sad eyes.

He slammed a weak hand against the wood slats of the porch. "Armin, how did you get here?" he repeated with more intensity.

Armin crawled across the grass, cringing with pain. He reached the bottom step before he collapsed. "Stella," he whimpered. "It was Stella. She used me. Used Stone."

"I know all about that," growled Benjamin. "I know she married him. And you. I also know they started a mining operation. One you took over at some point. What on earth were you thinking, Armin?"

"It was Stella," Armin repeated. "Stone died just a few months after they started Penstone. Stella said she needed a- a figurehead?" He shook his head. "Whatever that is. Said she couldn't do it without a man. Made me marry her even though I hated her. I ran the company for her, did what she told me, and we made a lot of money."

"It nearly destroyed the town," the professor accused, stepping forward.

"I didn't know what I was doing," Armin answered. "I just did what I was told. Soon enough she decided she'd gotten all she could from the mines. She wanted to leave Saint's Grove but I didn't want to go." He squeezed his eyes shut, tears escaping the corners. "So she did something to me. Turned me into a monster. Sent me to live in the woods. Said I had to stay there and I would never die until I could right my wrongs. Even now, after you stabbed me with that knife, I can't die. I don't even know how I changed back to my human form, but either way, I'll live with the pain until my wound heals, but I'll never die." He shook his head. "There's no way to right the wrongs I've done."

"Why did you attack us?" Professor McGurty asked. "You could have killed Irene."

"She came back," Armin moaned. "Didn't look like her, but it was her. She found me in the woods a couple days ago. Told me that terrible people were plotting against her and to find the woman that lived in my family home and stop her. I can only come out at night, though, and that was the first chance I had to get at you." He gave Irene a mournful expression. "I'm glad you stopped me. I didn't want to do it. I just couldn't stop myself. I could see what I was doing and I hated myself for it."

"She's a witch," Benjamin ground out. "A terrible, evil witch. She must have cursed you like she cursed me. She's responsible for my death."

Armin moaned, one hand running through his hair. "I know." He squeezed his eyes shut as tears leaked out the side. "I was there," he whispered.

"What?" Benjamin hissed. "What the hell do you mean you were there?"

Armin whimpered, recoiling a little at Benjamin's fierceness. "I couldn't help it, brother!" he cried. "She did

197

something to me. Changed me. I didn't want to do it, but she gave me the mask and the knife."

"No. Oh, no." Irene wrapped her arms around Benjamin, gripping him even tighter as she realized what Armin was telling them.

Benjamin sank against her, all the color draining from his face. "What are you trying to tell me?"

Armin held out a hand, reaching for his brother. "I didn't want to, Benjamin, I swear it. I couldn't stop myself."

"It was you?" Benjamin whispered. "You were the man behind the mask?"

Armin nodded. "She laughed, Benjamin. She thought it was funny, even while I cried and cried!" he wailed, tears falling freely down his face.

Benjamin let out a ferocious roar filled with all the hurt and agony in his soul.

"Oh, dear," Professor McGurty murmured, coming to kneel beside Irene. He placed a hand on Benjamin's shoulder.

"Please, brother," Armin keened. "I know I can never make up for what I did. For letting her do what she did to me. But if you forgive me, maybe I can forgive myself someday."

Tears flowed down Benjamin's cheeks. "I would have died for you, Armin."

Armin began to keen loudly, his hands balling into fists. He crawled up the porch, a trail of blood following him. "I can never make up for what I did," he gasped in pain, reaching for Benjamin. "Telling you I'm sorry will never be good enough."

Irene felt as though her heart were breaking as she

watched the two brothers. "Benji," she pleaded, not really sure what she was asking for.

Benjamin seemed to understand, however, and he leaned forward toward his brother. He stayed that way for several long moments, a muscle in his jaw ticking slightly before he finally let out a deep, shuddering sigh and took Armin's hand in his. "It wasn't your fault, Armin," he told his brother. "Stella was an evil witch and she cast a spell over you long before she cursed you to live as you have the last hundred and forty years, long before she cursed my soul to an eternity of limbo. You couldn't help it."

Armin's eyes shimmered as he looked at his brother. "Does that mean …?"

"If ever you needed my forgiveness, you have it," Benjamin told him, squeezing his hand tightly.

Armin shuddered as tears of relief coursed down his cheeks. He relaxed against the porch. "You've always been too good to me," he sighed.

"No, brother," Benjamin choked out. "You were a good man, a good brother. Don't ever let her take that away from you. I love you."

Armin sighed again. "I love you too, Benjamin." His body seemed to relax even more, and after a moment, a faint light began to emanate from him.

"What's happening?" Irene asked.

The light grew brighter, stronger and stronger until Armin seemed to be made of nothing but the light like a tiny sun.

"Armin?" Benjamin asked sharply. "Are you okay?"

Armin didn't answer and Professor McGurty chuckled softly. "Don't you see?" he turned to them. "He had to right his wrongs. It didn't matter that he wasn't responsible, or that the witch forced him to kill you. His guilt has kept him here. Your forgiveness has set him free."

Benjamin swallowed hard, tears coursing down his face as he watched his brother's body as it seemed to dissolve, breaking apart and filling the night air like thousands of fireflies. They drifted into the sky, fading away as they went, and just before the last one disappeared, they heard Armin's voice one more time.

"Thank you, brother."

Benjamin pulled Irene against him, his tears wetting her shirt. She rocked him in her arms. "Shh," she soothed. "At least you know what happened to him. And he's at peace now."

She reached up to run her hand through his hair when the sound of the first dingdong of a church bell filled the air. She froze, her eyes meeting those of the professor.

He met her gaze. "It's midnight," he cried as the bell rang again. He jumped off the porch and grabbed the Star Anthame off the ground, throwing it to her. She caught it deftly in one hand.

The bell rang a third time.

"Benjamin!" she cried, tears streaming down her face.

He hugged her tightly as the bell rang again.

"I love you," he uttered fiercely, kissing her once. The bell rang a fifth time.

"I love you too," she sobbed.

The bell struck a sixth time.

"You have to do it," the professor called to them. "Before it's too late!"

Dong! The bell rang again, and Irene wailed. "I can't!"

"You have to," Benjamin insisted. "We have to break

the power of the Anthame."

The church bell rang again and Irene shook her head.

"Please," Benjamin begged. "You have to."

"Benji, I'm sorry," she wept as the bell rang again. She lifted the Anthame in a trembling hand, poising it over his chest. The bell rang for the tenth time.

"Do it!" he yelled. "Now, Irene!"

The bell struck again and Irene screamed as she brought the knife down, plunging it into his chest. Bright light burst forth from the wound, shooting off in all directions as Benjamin cried out. His back arched high off the wooden slats of the porch, and the light faded. He collapsed and lay still.

The bell rang a final time and then all grew quiet. A moment later, Irene and the professor watched as bright lights began shooting up into the sky from various parts of town. The rift was sealing itself and taking others with it.

One of those lights erupted in front of them, hovering in front of the porch for a moment. Irene shaded her eyes, but after a moment they adjusted and she gasped when she saw her father standing in the center.

Professor McGurty gasped. "Joseph!"

Joseph Bell smiled. "Hey, old friend. It's good to see you again."

The professor smiled, his eyes shining with unshed tears. "And you as well. I always knew you didn't run off."

"No," he shook his head before turning to Irene. "You did good, my dear. I'm proud of you."

Irene wept. "I don't feel like I did good. I feel terrible."

"Don't worry, daughter. All will be as it should." He

glanced over his shoulder, before turning back to her. "I have to go now." A great smile crossed his face. "Your mother is calling to me."

He hovered for a moment until he seemed to dissolve into the light and it shot straight up into the night sky. After his light disappeared, a few more followed, but soon there were no more lights and the night seemed to settle, feeling normal for the first time in a week.

Finally alone, Irene and the professor turned back to the porch. She stood for a moment, looking at the man she loved lying motionless and then she let out a painful cry that filled the night air before she collapsed next to him, sobbing helplessly.

"Irene." The professor laid a gentle hand on her shoulder.

"No!" she swiped his hand away, barely able to speak. "How can I go on knowing what I've done?"

"*Irene,*" he insisted. "Look."

She lifted her head, her vision blurred with tears. She wiped them away to find him pointing toward the sky. She followed the direction of his finger and saw a warm glow descending from the heavens. It drifted toward them until it hovered over the porch. A moment later it settled over Benjamin like a blanket, covering his entire body, seeping into him.

A faint sliver of hope coursed through Irene.

He stirred and the sliver erupted into joy.

She gathered him into her arms. "Benjamin?"

His eyes fluttered, then opened. He smiled when he saw her and lifted a hand to cup her cheek. "Sweet girl."

A hoarse cry broke free from her lips and she pressed her lips against his. "How?" she wept. "Oh, how?"

"I told you before," he murmured between kisses. "All will turn out as it should. You should have listened. I'm a very smart man."

Irene pulled away, laughing, turning to see the professor smiling down at them, tears running down his cheeks as well.

"Can you stand?" the old man asked. "Can you leave the bookstore?"

Irene helped Benjamin up, and he moved down the steps, hesitating on the last one. He took a deep breath and stepped down onto the grass.

They all waited for several long, tense moments, but finally it became apparent that he was going nowhere.

Benjamin broke out in a grin so joyful, his companions couldn't help grinning back. "I'm a person again!" he quipped.

Irene laughed. "You were always a person to me."

He scooped her up in his arms, spinning her around before setting her on the ground in front of him. "You saved me, my sweet girl. How can I ever thank you?"

She put her hands on either side of his face. "I only want one thing from you," she told him. "Just love me. For the rest of my life."

"Done," he declared, just before his lips captured hers.

One Year Later

Irene stood on the little balcony off her bedroom, looking out on the town square. A short distance away she watched Anika and Isaac talking to Flora and Professor McGurty, all of them seated at a picnic table covered in food.

Try as she might, she'd never been able to force herself to call the professor Mycroft, but it didn't stop her from loving him any less. She was ecstatic that he had found happiness with Flora.

Anika had become a dear friend, and Isaac had turned into the perfect companion for Benji.

Benji. He sat at the table with them, laughing and smiling. He must have felt her eyes on him, however, because a moment later he glanced up at her and blew her a kiss.

Warmth filled her as she waved at her husband.

Her husband.

They had been married less than two months after the eclipse, and now, on the anniversary of the event, the friends had come together to celebrate their good fortune.

After Benjamin had come back to her, they had disassembled the Star Anthame, returning the stone to Liam and Albert. The hilt went back in the museum with Mark and Lisa, and just to make sure it could never be used again, they melted the blade down.

Benjamin had been spending as much time with the professor as he could, learning about his new world. The professor had helped him get a job at the college as his assistant, so he had something to fill his days.

Yes, good fortune had touched them, and would continue to do so, she was certain.

Benjamin waved at her. "Are you coming down?" he hollered up at her, and the others turned to beckon her as well.

She smiled. "I'll be right there," she called.

Her hand drifted down and caressed her flat stomach for a moment. "What do you think, little one?" she whispered. "Is now the right time to tell them?"

She needed no answer, however, as she had been planning this day for weeks. Benjamin would be the best father in the world, and she couldn't wait to tell him.

She turned to hurry down the stairs and out the front door.

Her life waited for her out there. Not inside, in her store, or hidden in a book somewhere. No, it was outside, with the people she loved and nestled deep in her womb.

"Thank you," Irene said to no one in particular as she hurried across the square. "Thank you for everything."

The End

Continue on for a sneak preview of the next book in
the Saint's Grove series,

All Dragons' Eve

by Casse NaRome

ALL DRAGONS' EVE

CASSE NAROME

Ana Benten spent her life dreaming of something bigger for herself. After high school graduation, she leaves Saint's Grove in the hopes of finding what will make her truly happy. But even the best-laid plans are no guarantee. When her grandmother passes, Ana's life comes full-circle. She's forced to return home and accept what life has thrown at her. The last thing she ever imagined she'd have to accept, arrives in the form of a handsome stranger who barrels into the jewelry shop she inherited, just in time to save her.

Ka-Riu knows what it's like to have your life turned up-side down in the blink of an eye. On what was supposed to be an ordinary day, spent soaring through the skies with his siblings, Ka-Riu and his people find themselves trapped in a curse—in another dimension, in human form. The only way to reverse the curse and gain his life back is to find the stones and the Bentaizen Goddesses who can assist his people. He is on a mission to not let his family down.

Strangely drawn to this mysterious man, Ana volunteers to help the legendary Ka-Riu. Could saving the dragons be the key to finally realizing where she belongs and set her on her true path? With the clock ticking and destiny impatiently waiting, their joining of forces has the potential to change countless lives, especially their own. Will the new path they set lead to Ana finally embracing her true destiny and living the life she fought so hard to attain with the dragon that has undeniably fallen for her?

Chapter One

Ka-Riu

My gaze focused on the flames dancing in front of me, then anxiously toward the darkened sky. It was almost time and the closer the planets were to alignment, the more my body yearned to catch fire and take flight. My fingers tingled with the need to molt and leave this earth-bound form. Three hundred and fifty years and I still hadn't grown accustomed to how limiting gravity made my human form feel.

Fuku stood at the door, tapping his tan Johnson and Murphys. "Are you sure that you want to do this?"

I shot him a look. "Why wouldn't I want to do it?"

"Our entire race depends on this. More importantly, our family's future depends on this." Fuku leaned down and brushed soot off the tip of his shoe.

I stood up and walked over to the gilded mirror and checked my appearance one more time. My dark auburn hair flickered bronze in the fire light. "Thanks for the enormous vote of confidence, big bro."

"You just miss blazing up the night skyline like you are the second sunrise."

I smiled at the memory. Goddess I did miss that!

"Are you going across dressed like that?" Fuku asked,

interrupting my pretend flight. I could almost feel Sui's rain rolling over my flaming scales.

"The fuck you mean? What's wrong with what I'm wearing?" I looked down at my designer jeans and sky blue button down. I mean yes, the jeans had a few holes but nothing extreme. I didn't look homeless or anything.

He shook his head.

"I'm going to wear that leather coat over it." I offered.

"Because *that* makes it better."

He looked utterly disgusted. "No time to change now." He looked up at the darkened sky as the planets aligned and a globe of light itched across the sky.

"It's about time," I said around a gulp.

I watched as Fuku inspected my face. "You'll do fine."

I nodded but the nerves kept me from speaking.

"Want me to go? I can do this. There is still time for you to change your mind if you want me to do it for you. I don't mind. We can tell everyone I insisted. I am the oldest; you must bow to my will."

I laughed. "Like that will ever happen." I appreciated his offer.

"They are coming. Last chance."

I shrugged into my coat and I could hear him gag. Seriously, I didn't look that bad. We all couldn't be as suave and debonair as he was.

"Let's do this."

Chapter Two

Ana

It was going to be a good night. The town was bustling with anxious excitement as residents claimed their spots in the town square. It was always like this when there was an event. In Saint's Grove, we love a good celebration. I mean I enjoyed it for different reasons than most, I'm sure. Nobody would be coming into my shop. Who wants to buy necklaces or any other bauble when they could watch planets do planet things?

I had my music turned up just loud enough that I could channel my inner riot girl, so all my responsibility didn't make me feel too old.

I pulled the last box to inventory towards me. These were the stones Victor sent from some far off land, I'm sure. He was really geeked about this lot. He had called it a find. I laughed. He always got so excited. Every single lot is his best yet. There was no, "Eh I've seen better ", with him. I think it was maybe his best quality. The guy loved playing in the dirt.

I looked down at my inventory sheet. No. No, no, no; this couldn't be right. I looked around again at all the previously opened boxes. Shit! These were no way all the boxes that I was supposed to have. That means some lazy jerk decided he wanted to cut out from work early instead of doing all his deliveries. What really pissed me off was they thought giving me half would keep me from noticing.

I pushed up from the floor lifting the box and category sheets with me. Why did people insist on trying to derail my night?

I carried the heavy box filled with various rocks to the cluttered desk where the old fashioned phone sat. I flipped through the rolodex; yes, the store still used one. Grandma refused to enter the millennium and I hadn't gotten around to it when she passed away.

I punched the number and took a deep breath to calm my rage.

"Calvin!" I barked into the phone as soon as he said hello. I guess my breathing exercises hadn't worked.

"Ana, what's up? You barely caught me. We were heading out to watch the lunar eclipse," the current bane of my existence informed me, sounding oh so nonchalant.

"I'm missing the rest of my order, man. My guess is about five or six boxes worth of it."

"Hold on, let me check—"

"Don't pull that with me. I know that you know damn well you have my boxes," I said, trying not to scream.

I heard him trying to muffle the phone receiver. "Junior, check if we have any boxes for Benten."

Didn't I just say not to try this shit on me? They should feel lucky I was trying to turn over a new leaf—a nicer, calmer one that didn't include going around cussing folks out and punching them in their stupid mouths.

"Shit, I'm sorry, Ana. They were mixed in with tomorrow's deliveries. We will get them to you first thing." He rushed, trying to hurry me off the phone from the speed of his words.

"No, that is not acceptable. What am I supposed to do tonight without those boxes to inventory? This is holding up my work. I need to do this tonight because I have designing tomorrow. I should not still be inventorying stock. That is why we paid for delivery today; so guess what? I want the delivery today." I finished with my free hand flailing to punctuate my point. I am sure I looked like a crazy woman.

"Look, Ana—"

"Don't you 'look, Ana' me! You, look, you are a business and your job is to make the customer happy. I spend a lot of money with you guys, I am a customer and guess what? I am *not* happy. Make me happy, Calvin. There are a bunch of other shipping companies. I'd hate to have to take my business elsewhere; or that I even have to threaten it, but you are holding up my process."

"Ana, do what you have to do? The entire town is shutting down for this event. Take the night off and mingle with your neighbors."

"Calvin—"

The phone went silent. I groaned and slammed the phone back in its cradle.

"Now what?" I asked the room full of boxes and crates. I tapped my fingers on the only un-inventoried box. I could finish up tomorrow and go rub elbows with the towns-folk today. I laughed. That was not going to happen. I had basically been run out of here with pitchforks fifteen years ago. No way in hell was I close to ready to play nice with these people.

Bad enough I was once again stuck in this town. I could always sell the shop, pack back up and hit the road.

I could almost hear my Grandma's snort of disgust. Not only would she tell me that I was actually my own problem and *not* the neighbors. Which, may or may not be the truth. She would also remind me of the actual facts.

I was stuck here and I couldn't sell this place. The curse of being the sole remaining Benten—this was my birth right.

My cellphone rang and I peeked at the caller ID.

"Hey, Mama." I tried to fight back my sigh. How did she always know when I needed her, but would never admit it?

"Oshun, what's the matter?" My mother asked.

I shook my head, even though she was half the world away.

"Nothing is wrong, Mama, just this damn jewelry shop and people's complete incompetence." I semi-confessed, while absentmindedly pulling labeled bundles from the box in front of me.

Her warm chuckle crossed the distance and it found my heart, causing it to soar. "Jemma must have gone insane in her last days to think you had the temperament for that place."

"Right," my laugh joined Mama's over the connection. "I so do not have any of her sainted patience for this. I'm going to end up ripping someone's head off."

"You always had the temper of a dragon, daddy used to say." Mom's tone pitched in sorrow-filled longing.

I knew how much she missed my dad. I missed him too. The pain of his absence was so tangible; at times I could almost reach out and hold the aching. Wow, it was now only mom and I left in the family. Once she was gone, I'd be all alone. I mean *alone,* alone.

"You could find a boyfriend," she offered.

"Ma, you know I hate when you do that. It creeps me out." It was my age old whine.

"Do what?" I could hear the teasing in her tone.

"Don't act like you don't know." I had to really hold in the foot stomp.

"I can't read your mind. You are just easy to know."

"Did you need something?" I asked just to change the subject. I was not easy to read. Mom always did that and I wasn't the only one she could do it with either. She had the uncanny ability to know exactly what other people were thinking.

"You are my daughter—my only child, Oshun. I don't need a reason to call you, do I?" She was trying to guilt me.

I forced my eyes not to roll because she'd know.

"How is Gran-Gran? 'She okay?" I asked about her mother.

"Oh, you know that woman's going to live forever."

I sure hoped she did. With her, I wouldn't be so alone; even if she were in another continent across huge bodies of water. Hell, if I were so lonely about it, maybe I should try to stop being a bitch and make friends. I mean I had Paola. I've always had her. We'd been friends since we were kids. I'd even managed to keep in touch with her after high school when I high-tailed it from Saint's Grove.

"Oshun are you listening to me?" I heard my mom huffing when I finally pulled myself from my thoughts.

"It's Ana. Yes, I am listening," I lied. "And Mama would you please stop calling me that?" I pleaded.

Her sigh was so very put upon. It was the kind of heavy that always made me feel instantly guilty. "Baby doll, you can run from a lot of things, but never can you run from the truth. Especially when it from who you are."

I barked laughter. Hell, I wasn't even sure who I was to run from it. I am thirty-four years old and still had no idea what the hell I was doing. I mean, I know I didn't want to sit still or be tied down. But even with all the moving and traveling I'd done for the past decade, it still felt like that was what I was doing. I couldn't help but feel as if I was stuck in this holding pattern I called life. I was surrounded by strangers constantly. I know for a fact that very few people got along with me; or could even stand me for that matter. Mama and Paola were the beginning and the end of that list. I'm not going to point any fingers on who was to blame either.

Dating was out. Most guys wanted a little missus to conform to society's ideal of what life should be. You say, I do, pop out a few crumb snatchers to chase after while hubby chases after something else completely and that was supposed to make a girl feel whole. Yeah, no thanks—I'll take a hard pass.

"Mama, I'm not running. It's more like I'm searching," I admitted.

"For what? Would you know if you find it?" She sighed again and I could practically visualize her settling back as she prepared to dig in. I knew once she started I couldn't stop her.

"Sometimes, when you stop moving, what you are seeking will find you. While you are moving, looking for what you think you are missing, what you need can't catch up. If you keep running from only you know what, you are also running from your future. Be still for a while and you'll be surprised at what you catch."

I nibbled on my bottom lip and pushed my hair from my face as I mulled over Mama's advice. The weight of my emptiness crushed down on my shoulders as I gulped down the lump in my throat and I fought tears. I willed my voice to be clear.

"I just feel so aimless, Ma. I'm not a kid anymore. I don't know when that happened exactly. When I went from twenty-young to thirty-lost years old but it did." I leaned into my phone, yearning for my mother's hug. "Sometimes, there comes a point you have to accept what life is offering you; whether you want it or not. You have to realize that maybe the cause of all your problems are you."

"Oshun—"

"No, Mama. It's the truth. I'm just going to stay here and live other people's dreams for me. I'm going to run Obaasan's shop, go to school and finish college, and make some kind of life here. I can be happy here. I mean, it won't be a cookie cutter version of society's force-fed dream, but it will be a happiness I can stomach."

"I think a person can be happy anywhere but there might be bigger things for you. Don't you dare settle; you deserve more than you realize. You *are* more than you realize. But I think a part of you knows that fact; maybe that is why you are so restless. We are a family of strong women with a stronger legacy that all comes down to you. You may very well be the last in my family's line, as you are in your father's—no, I won't *bingo* you or your choice to be childfree. But that leaves a lot on your shoulders. I think you are strong enough; Gran-Gran and Jemma do as well. You'll be fine. You have your ancestors on your side. Your father and I both have such diverse, yet equally remarkable, histories and it all flows through you. Remember that."

Mom had never said anything this intense to me before and it took me a moment to compose myself.

"Uh, thank you, Ma." I swallowed the lump in my throat. Her words had managed to cut through the icy bullshit I always kept people at bay with.

"Are you going to the viewing of the planets aligning and lunar eclipse? It's almost time, right?"

"Yes, it's about that time; but no, I am not going. I'm going to keep working and enjoy the calm. Hopefully, I will get a lot of work done and get ahead of schedule."

Even in her silence I could freaking hear her disappointment. How does she do this to me? Only she had the ability to make me feel this guilty when I wasn't doing anything wrong.

"Thank you for calling me, Mama. It really helped. More than you know," I offered, ignoring her weighty judgment.

"Not a problem. Be careful, my brave Oshun. Be careful." The line went silent and I shook my head before taking my cell from my ear then placing it back in my pocket. I cranked the volume on the stereo higher, to blast my exposed emotions away. Booty shaking was quick to follow as the bass pounded through my body.

Still wiggling my backside, I made my way over to look at the Orders Due Log for the next piece for me to finish. I dug in my supply drawers and pulled out the kits needed. This was going to be a quick commission— simple copper washed arm cuff with chrysocolla beaded inset.

Pulling on my headband magnifier glass loupe, I took my seat in my workspace. The same workspace Jemma had used all her years here. As a girl, I remember watching her sit in this exact spot as her fingers worked, fluttered and twirled the metal into a work of wearable art. Then as a teenager, I still used to come in to help her and pretend I hated every moment of it, while sneaking peeks at her performing her version of magic.

Calm came over me as my fingers did the same smooth dance as grandma's over the beads to pick out the correct size and shape by feel alone. This was the part of running the shop I loved. Forget the customer service and the jacked up deliveries; making jewelry and being able to work with the special gifts the Earth yields to us was pure bliss.

It was my job to make art for someone who would yearn to wear it. My creation on display. I picked three perfect stones. They were perfect for their imperfections in the way humans would never be able to claim.

The music set the rhythm of the hammering to the copper band I was distressing.

Screams cut through the music, throwing off my pace. I stopped banging dents into the sturdy cuff pushing the lens of my loupe up, willing my ears to cut through the music. I could barely make out the sound of swift foot falls from the windows at the store front.

Reaching over to kill the music the ground erupted in violent tremors, the walls threatened to buckle as the shelves rattled vigorously against the floor.

"Holy shit." I hit the power button ending my rage fest. Was that an earthquake? I mean no shit but, really? Did Saint's Grove have earthquakes? Had an abandoned mine collapsed?

I darted toward the archway that would take me to the

front of the store as I ranted. "If they'd started digging for oil and triggered those damn fracking quakes I'm going to kick somebody's ass!"

When I entered the open room, I stopped in my tracks—chaos. That was the only way to describe what was unfolding before my eyes outside my windows.

The bell chimed as someone rushed in through the front door. A tall willowy guy quickly shut the door after him and peeked through the glass. He must have not liked what he witnessed. He frowned.

Hard flesh slammed against me in a tackle that threw me off balance, knocking me to the floor. Glass exploded around us. Shards of it raining down around me in sharp splinters, warmth covered me as the stranger attempted to shield me as best he could.

What seemed like an eternity later, with my heart thumping the entire time, the weight that pinned me lifted. I watched him shake slivers and clumps of glass from himself.

Without warning his eyes landed on me. The room instantly grew claustrophobic. His brown eyes, warming me like fire and my cheeks flushed in response. He smelled like a campfire and I was suddenly very aware of how much I've always liked the scent.

"Thank you for not struggling. Are you injured? Did I hurt you?" His voice was smooth and creamy, covering every inch of me like a balm.

"I think, I'm fine," I croaked out, pulling myself into a sitting position. He reached a hand out in an offer of assistance. I wasn't too proud to accept it. His grip was pure restrained strength and with a quick yank, I was on my feet with zero effort of my own.

For some odd reason, I couldn't pull my stare from his hand. They were lined with small scratches from the glass shower he had protected me from. He gently tugged his hand from mine, pulling me from my trance in the process. I hadn't even realized I was still holding onto it. I looked up into his face, embarrassed. He gave a small smile before he went back over to the busted out window and ducked his head out the newly formed hole.

My fucking store. I groaned. I was going to have to get this fixed as soon as possible and with all the incompetence going around that would probably take forever. *This is fantastic*, I lamented to myself while looking around at the damage.

"We need to get somewhere safe," the man spoke as he turned back to face me.

"We?"

"We either have to secure all these windows or get out of here if we want to remain alive," he continued as if I hadn't said a word.

"Remain alive? Kind of dramatic don't you think? Who the hell are you?" I rushed over to him, in order to get a look at what he saw. "What the heck is going on out there? A riot?"

I mean, I can say a lot of negative things about my hometown, but they weren't the rioting kind.

"Holy shit. *Holy shit!* What's going on?" I could feel the panic rising up inside me. Was this even real? My body trembled as I caught sight of something I couldn't even begin to rationalize. Oh god.

A strong arm wrapped around my waist and pulled me from the hole, guiding me until I was facing him; his body was between me and the windows. His eyes locked onto mine once more, snapping me out of my near hysteria.

"Act now, freak out later," I scolded myself and he raised a brow, the corner of his mouth quirking up.

I had no time to freeze or ball up in a corner and cry over the shit I just saw. If this was Armageddon, and to be honest I'm sure to hell that's what I witnessed, I was going to need to keep my shit together.

Step one, protect *Obaasan's* shop.

"Move away from the windows and stay still for a second." I ducked behind the counter and activated the security system. The mesh and bars lowered down over the large display windows of the store front. The stranger backed away from the door, his eyes tracking me as I took the keys and turned the lock, pulled down the security door and locked that as well.

"I did not expect all this to happen." The stranger's voice cut through the new silence cause by the metal blocking out most of the unleashed noise out in the courtyard of the town square.

"Should I be out there helping people?" I questioned myself over my decision to lock the door before going out and attempting to bring people into safety with me.

The guy answered my question. "In order to save others, you must first make sure you are safe."

I narrowed my eyes at him. Right. "First things first, since I have maybe stupidly locked myself in with you. Who are you?"

He grinned. "Sorry. I'm Ka-Riu."

I stared at him as he looked at me like I was supposed to recognize him or maybe the name. I shook my head. Nothing.

"I came to pick up something that I was told Jemma would have for me. Are you Jemma? Is she here?" He looked around the store as if someone else were hiding around here somewhere.

I snapped out of it. Of course, he was a customer of Jemma's. "Uh no. I'm not Jemma, I'm her grand-daughter, Ana. My Grandmother passed away over a year ago."

I started to cover up the jewels and lock the cases be-fore setting the alarm in my meticulous process to distract myself from the awkwardness I always felt when I had to inform a customer of Jemma's death. I always felt the need to offer them my condolences when I was the once she was related to. But honestly, they probably knew her better than I did, since over the last ten years when I was flitter-ing about like a bee, they were here with her.

"She-she. I mean Jemma is—" Ka-Riu raked his hand through his dark auburn hair. "I-I don't know what—" He finally stopped trying as he leaned against the wall in what I would guess was defeat.

"I'm sorry. Were you close to her?" I took a step to-ward him, to give him comfort before forcing myself to stop. What the hell, Ana.

His head slowly looked up from his despair, our eyes locked and my heart more than missed its next beat. His eyes narrowed as he tilted his head. I watched him take me in and I could feel everywhere his eyes landed. They final-ly settled back on my eyes. I should say something, but the silence had stretched on so long it might as well last forev-er. I decided to do my own appraisal of the man in front of me.

His legs were long and he really knew how to wear jeans. They sat low on his narrow hips, draping loose in pleasing lines down his thighs until they fell over his stylish sneakers. The small holes didn't look bought but well-worn, as if they were his favorite pair. They looked soft and I could imagine rubbing my palm across them. The light blue shirt under his leather jacket also looked soft as it stretched across his lean chest. Like him, I once more settled my gaze back to his eyes that almost had the same slight tilt in the corners as mine. I raised my brow in a silent question, *how do* you *like being checked out too*?

There was a thump at the back door and Ka-Riu's posture shot straight. "I need to go make sure everything is secure back there. Do you mind?"

Before I answered, he was strolling through the archway. Shortly after, furniture scraped against the floor. Minutes later he came back into the room whipping sweat from his brow, his smooth hands swift in the task, as if he didn't want me to see that the task took that much effort from him.

Wait, smooth? I could have sworn he had been cut. I walked over to him and grabbed on to one of his wrist and inspected one hand, then repeated with the other. "What happened to your scratches?"

He looked at me like I was insane but didn't answer.

"From the glass, you had—"

"What are you wearing on your head?" His voice sounded amused. "I've been trying to ignore it but, seriously, what is that." He reached out to touch it.

Crap. I'm sure I *did* look insane. "It's a loupe. I use it for making jewelry. I got distracted when you came in and forgot to take it off." I whipped it from my head and tossed the band on the nearest counter.

"Here is what is happening." He came and stood in

front of me, propping his elbow on the glass between us.

I swatted him off before he continued.

"My family sent me here to pick up something very important to us. Jemma was supposed to have it ready for today." He spoke in a weird unrecognizable accent. I assumed he was of Asian descent from his appearance alone. From his features I would say he was Japanese but his high crest speech pattern didn't match.

"Well, if she had an order for you it would have been classified as either, paid and unclaimed or unclaimed commissions uncomp." I moved over to the far display case. "Do you have the order receipt?" I held out my hand. Ka-Riu followed me and stopped once more in front of me.

"I don't think it was paid for. I don't see how it would be, it was kind of a long standing verbal thing between our families." He reached his fingers as if to tap against the glass. I halted him with a sharp glance.

"Okay, then it would have been put in the resell commissions." I unlocked the case and pulled the black velvet covering from it.

I watched his eyes flickering over every piece until he reached the very end. His shoulders slumped.

"It's not there." The corners of his mouth fell in a perfect caricature of a sad face.

"That's okay." My voice softened in an effort to comfort him with reassurance. "Maybe it has already sold."

"How is that better?" He groaned.

"Because, if it sold, we can track it down. One more option. I can find out who bought it or where it currently is because Grandma kept perfect records of her orders, verbal or otherwise. Maybe it will be in there. If she was supposed to have it for you, no doubt she documented it."

I covered the display and secured it once more. "Hand me those binders over there." I pointed before continuing to make sure everything was back in its place.

He dumped the old binders filled with grandma's small and tight handwriting on the counter as gently as he could. Don't think I didn't notice the pointed look he shot me either.

"Grandma was super meticulous with her notes on her orders. If she had something for your family, then rest assured it is in here somewhere." I opened up the pages and the sight of what was left of whom my grandma was caused a lump to form in my throat. I smoothed my hand over the page slowly, hoping to feel any bit of her.

"Are you alright, Ana?" He dipped his head to look into my eyes. Concern creased the space between his brows.

"Uh—so. I—yes. I'm great." I cleared my throat. "Thanks for asking. Anyway, they are alphabetical. What's your last name?"

"It's Riu. R-i-u. Or sometimes spelled R-y-u if she was old school."

I started to flip through the first book. Ka-Riu grabbed another one and began to look through that one. I closed mine and moved through the next in the pile. There was another loud noise outside and Ka-Riu made sure he was directly between me and the sound without stopping his search through the binders.

"Anything in that one?" I asked as he reached for another one. It was a dumb question but I had to ask just to give me something to say.

"Nothing." He flipped through to the R section and I

peeked over to see. He must have felt me over the shoulder reading because he turned his attention to me. I smiled as if I wasn't annoying.

He put his index finger on my forehead and gently pushed me away. "Your binder is way over there." His laugh was evident in his words.

"I was just trying to help," I lied.

He shook his head. "Sure. I think I can handle searching for my own name."

I laughed. "Fine."

"What was it like to have Jemma as your grandmother?" He asked, changing the subject.

My grin grew wider. How did he know that I'd been thinking about her? Maybe Mama was right and I was easy to read.

"Obaasan was great. I lived with her when my dad passed away when I was fifteen. She used to force me to come help her here after school every day until I graduated." I rolled my eyes. "Between you and me, I loved it. I hadn't seen her in years when one day I had the feeling that I needed to get home. Good thing I listened because a few months later, she died. That's how I got this place. She was my dad's mother and when she passed away I was the only one left to run the shop. She left everything to me so here I am."

He nodded. "Do you have any siblings?"

"Nope it's just me. My parents said I was more than enough. How about you?" I asked as I returned to my search.

"I wish it were just me. My mother had five kids and I'm the youngest." He looked completely pained.

"I always wondered what that would be like, to have

so many personalities constantly around. My house always seemed so silent and lonely. Oh! I found you," I exclaimed.

He almost jumped over the counter and knocked me out the way, he was so excited. He leaned forward just as I'd done to try and read it upside down.

I placed my entire palm on his face and pushed him back to his side, just as he had done to me earlier.

"See, that doesn't feel so nice, now does it?" I scolded as he playfully swatted my hand away. "I'll read it to you. Stay over there."

"Sorry. I got excited. This is very important to me. My entire family really and they are kind of trusting me to do this. Which is huge in itself."

My face fell. "Shit. I'm sorry but it's not good news," I warned. Feeling genuinely bummed for him. "It says, 'Ryu—Hearth Stone—order pending. Acquisition—in progress."

"Wha-what does that mean?" His voice was so small, bordering on helpless. I had a suspension he had an idea of exactly what it meant.

I walked around the counter until I was directly in front of him. I placed a hand on his forearm. "It means it isn't here. It never was. The stone is still being tracked down. But we can—"

There was a loud bang against the front door. I jumped, letting out a squeak. Ka-Riu quickly grabbed me and pulled me until I was tucked against his side.

"We have to get out of here." His hold on me didn't loosen.

"What is happening out there? I mean I saw… something. I can't explain what it was. Did something happen at the viewing?" I didn't want to admit it, but I was afraid to step foot out these doors and even though Ka-Riu was a complete stranger, I felt safe here.

"I will tell you all that I can; but first, I have to get you out of here. I hope it holds but I don't want to risk it." He turned to look at me and I'm not sure what he saw but his face softened and his arm tightened around me. "I will make sure you are safe."

I believed him.

"Okay, we need to leave sooner rather than later. Pack what you need to take and then we will go and find somewhere a bit safer." He finally released me.

I really didn't want to go out there, or anywhere near where that thing would possibly be. I looked at Ka-Rui and his face was set as he kept eye on the windows. I totally believed he wouldn't hesitate to do what he could to keep between me and danger. What I didn't know was *why*.

Chapter Three

Ka-Riu

I watched Ana turn in a small circle. It was slow and her eyes took in everything.

"Are you all right?" I narrowed my eyes in examination. Yet, she still kept rotating on the balls of her feet.

"I'm fine." Her voice was barely a whisper.

"You sure? I can help you pack while you do... that." Whatever *that* was. I mean, seriously, what the hell was she doing?

"Nah. I got this." She was still in her trance.

"Do you have anywhere we could go to be safe?" I pushed.

"Safe from what? I don't even know what the hell is going on and the thing I saw, nowhere is safe from that shit. Because that shit," she pointed over my shoulder, taking a moment from her slow pivot to do it, "is hell on Earth. So where exactly is safe from that?"

She started back her damn turning.

I threw my hands up. "Why are you doing that—what the hell are you doing, Ana?" I finally erupted.

She stopped once more and looked me square in the eyes. Hers were almond shaped, turned up slightly in the corners. They seemed to pin my soul. Heat flared through me and for an instant, if felt as if I'd molt and flame to life in my true form. I knew it wasn't possible but for a brief moment I almost believed it would happen.

"If this is the last time I'm in the shop, I want to take it all in. I know it sounds stupid to *you*. But this is all I have left of my family, okay! All my memories are here. So, if you would please just give me a damn minute!" She continued to pin me with a glare, but her voice softened. "Okay?"

"Okay," I repeated feeling about an inch tall. I felt like a complete asshole. "I didn't mean to try to rush you."

"Yeah, you did." She didn't sound angry, but she also wasn't letting me pull the foot from my mouth either.

"Fine, I did; but I'm sorry. How about I tell you what I know about what is happening out there while you get what you are taking together?" I negotiated, realizing I was still rushing her.

She shot me a look that made it clear that she hadn't missed that fact either.

"Fine," she relented.

I sighed in relief. I watched as she went over to the cash register and instead of pulling out cash, she pulled a small gun from its hiding spot. She checked a few things on it before lifting the cuff of her cream slacks exposing creamy peanut butter skin that looked satin smooth. I was only temporarily awarded the distraction before she slid the gun into place in a holster near her calf. Just before the leg of her pants fell back down, I got a peek of a fiery dragon tattoo. My heart thundered in my chest and once more flames sparked inside my core at the sight of the mark. I needed to get a hold of myself. She was a Benzaiten—the *last* Benzaiten to be exact, so I had no right lust-ing after her. The goddesses were able to mate dragons, but by all rights if she were the only one, Fuku was the one to have claim to her or any eldest of a clan. That thought made me want to eat my siblings, whole; and any other dragon that could possibly have claim to Ana.

I cringed. *What the fuck, man?* I had just met this girl and just because she flashed the bare minimal of skin, I was becoming undone. I shook my head. Maybe it was because I could still smell her and feel the soft skin of her palm from when she pressed it to my face. Her scent filled my nose and something came alive in me for the first time in, well since I hatched. Was it the goddess thing? Because holy *Tatsu*. Or maybe it was the tattoo that had done it. I never pictured her as the tattooed and packing heat type. I kind of liked the idea of a dragon that resembled me that closely marking her skin. Okay, I *really* liked that idea. I oddly liked that she knew her way around a .22, but a part of me hated that she might need to use it. If I could change forms, I would be better equipped to protect her because who needs a gun when you have a semi-tamed dragon?

"Are you ready?" She asked turning to face me. Now *she* was rushing *me*? I guess I had been having a whirl in my thoughts for a while.

"You are done?" I looked around because she'd only gotten her gun.

"That's all I need. Now you start explaining." Her expression basically told me that she was not going to let me weasel out of the promise.

"I'm not from here—"

"Obviously—" she interrupted.

"Ana, let me finish." I paused to see if she would comply. She mimed zipping her lips. She was absolutely adorable. I couldn't fight the smile that I knew spread over my face.

"I am not from here and I don't mean Saint's Grove or even Earth." I raised a hand silencing her before she even got started. "At least not *this* Earth. I'm from a place called Inventurea Prism. My people were banished there a very long time ago before I was born even. We have been waiting for this event for just as long. Somehow, it foolishly hadn't occurred to us that other dimensions might know about the coming events and be waiting as well. That was careless on our part."

I finally paused, allowing her an opportunity to reply.

She shook her head. "What?"

"Do you really want me to repeat it or was that a rhetorical 'what?'"

She didn't answer and I debated if I should go to her. But she possibly didn't want me near her since I just told her I was not from her Earth. All I could do was search her face for clues.

Was she going to lose it completely? I hope she didn't faint. I didn't really have time for human coddling. I also didn't have time to be entertained by how enchanting she looked from her bright eyes, perfect nose that was narrow— the bridge and fanned out slightly at the nostrils, the dip above the curve of her full lips with the lower one a bit more lush and both looked pillow soft. No, I totally did not have time for that or her hair that seemed to get curlier as time passed. Nope. No time. I had to get her out of here and in safety, then find that damn Hearth Stone before time ran out.

Yet, here I was, watching her as she crinkled her nose at the bridge as if she smelled something rancid. I realized it must be her thinking face and damned if it wasn't cute. My fingers tingled with the desire to reach out and trail one down the ridge of it to smooth it out. But I knew myself, if I gave in and touched her at that very moment, I would no longer be able to ignore her plush lips or her impossibly smooth skin. Like I was doing such a great job without laying a hand on her.

"You are from another dimension?" I jolted at the sound of her voice. I was thankful because my next stop was to check out the curve of her hips.

"Yes," I answered, adding a nod for something to do and to clear my thoughts to what was actually important. Not her body.

"Venturea Prisim. Why were you banished?" She went on.

I shook my head. "Too long of a story."

She didn't push, she only went on with her next question. "Why were you waiting for this day?"

"Due to the events that occurred tonight—the alignment of the stones, uh planets, the lunar eclipse, and the meteor shower— one crashed into the Earth at the exact moment and a tear or more like a hole between worlds. It is acting like a temporal portal." I grabbed a book of receipt paper and held a few up so they were all hanging down parallel. "These papers are different worlds. The celestial event tonight," I picked up scissors and poked holes through all the *dimensions* in a swift stab, one larger than the others. "The power of all those events at once caused the veil that keeps everything in its place and separate from one another, to rip. Now the beings from those other places can cross over at will until the universes correct themselves. This seems to be the place to be from what I saw out there."

"Beings, like that thing I saw out there, not human?" She gestured with her chin in the direction of the front door.

"No, some are humans. I mean I suppose some dimensions are merely different time points in the stream. But yes, a lot of the things I saw on my way to getting to you, they were not so much human."

"You aren't insane are you or pulling some sort of Halloween prank?" She asked, adding to her previous questions.

I shook my head. "No to both."

She grabbed the handle of the cabinet beside where she stood. When it opened, she removed a small backpack then took two small boxes of bullets and dumped them into the pack. I wanted to laugh but her reaction to her fear was respectable. I appreciated that her response could have been to freeze up but instead, she was the type to take action.

"I really don't think that will be necessary. I can protect you from all that is out there," I assured her. I wanted to believe that even in this form I still had the speed, strength and agility to keep the last Benzaiten Goddess safe.

"I want to believe you will try; but just in case, I need to be able to rely on me." She zipped up the bag.

I tried not to let that hurt. "We must get going."

"Which type of being are you, the human or the not so much?" She suddenly asked, as if it finally dawned on her that she should be worried.

"Promise you aren't going to use that on me?" I asked, nodding at where her calf holster was strapped. I let my tone drip with teasing. I knew that it would do me no harm. I would heal almost instantly from any bullet wound while I was in this form. If I were full dragon it wouldn't even penetrate the flaming scales.

"Depends. Besides, I make no promises or I'd end up letting a hell of a lot more people down than I already do." She folded her arms.

"None ever?" This time my teasing dipped into the flirtatious level against my will.

"I don't need to make that promise to you. Whatever your answer, I'm already pretty certain that you aren't a threat to me," she admitted while staring in my eyes; and at that moment, my heart might as well have ripped from my chest and fallen at her feet. I was hers and I knew I had no right to be.

I have heard the older dragons speak of the old magic. They told stories of fated bonds and how sudden it would hit the male and the pull that would rival any horde magic. It sucked that the object of my affection was completely inappropriate.

She was the last of the goddesses. She was going to be expected to reproduce to continue her line of dragon charmers. Once my family had possession of the Hearth stone, we'd not only be able to change into our dragon form once more, we'd be able to finally reproduce and Fuku would claim Ana to do just that. Even if I did by chance have a right to bond with her, I didn't want children. I never have and never would. I couldn't be the reason the dragon charmer lineage would end.

I gulped at the sadness that filled where my heart once beat.

"I am the latter," I finally admitted. I expected her to

retreat, but she didn't. I saw not a flicker of fear darken her expression. I was relieved. That would have fatally wounded me. Even without visible fear, I felt the need to offer her my vow.

"I happen to make promises and when I do, I never break them. Ana, I will never hurt you, nor will I allow anyone else to harm you. This is on my honor." I placed my left wrist over my heart in a full out pledge.

"Why not?" She finally spoke. "I mean I believe you but, why?"

My heart thumped hard as she crossed the room until she was standing in front of me. She smelled of Jasmine and Water Lilies. My back stiffened.

Oh, Goddess.

"We don't have time to get into that right now. Not here. We have to go." I should push her away from me. Her scent swirled around me and it was intoxicating. Who was I kidding? It would be pointless. The subtle scent of her would linger inside of me forever, no matter where she was on this Earth. I was screwed.

"I think we do have time since I will not move another inch until you," she poked a finger against my chest for emphasis. "Tell me what you are."

"A ghost, now let's go." I reached out and grabbed the hand that was at my chest and tugged. She didn't budge. I totally could have made her, but her words followed.

"No lies. I don't like being lied to. I get that you might be afraid of my reaction but if it helps I asked what you were and not who. I already have an idea of that. You can tell me you are just about anything and I'd think no less of you because from the moment you walked through that door you have done nothing but try to protect me. That is who you are."

I released her hand, but she held on to mine.

"Don't freak out. I'm a Draca."

Her blank stare met my timid one. Fine. Screw beating around the bushes.

"Draca means dragon. I'm a freaking Dragon, all right?"

Her grip tightened around my hand. "That's okay, I like dragons," she assured me softly.

"I kind of figured that when I saw the tattoo," I whispered.

She laughed. "Okay, I know it's a bit basic but in my defense, I got that when I was twenty-one."

"No, I like it. Not every day I meet a girl with a tattoo that looks almost exactly like me."

She let my hand go and hers flew to cover her mouth as she backed away from me. "No, it doesn't. Please tell me you are kidding?"

I shook my head. "Nope. Down to the fire and everything."

She covered her face. "This is kind of embarrassing. I swear, only I have this kind of humiliating luck."

"No, I find it flattering," I admitted.

"Of course you would! Who wouldn't want to meet a strange psycho with a tattoo of a dragon that happens to look like—" she groaned. "Ka-Riu!"

"Yes? What's wrong?" I rushed over to her.

"No. *Ka-Riu!* My grandmother gave me a book about dragons when I was sixteen and I loved it. How did I not recognize the name? I'm an idiot. I mean, of course I wouldn't put Ka-Riu the dragon and Ka-Riu the guy standing in my shop as one in the same, but seriously! I read that book so many times and I like the one who could light up the night sky with his scales of fire. That's the tattoo I got. I even took the book in so the guy could replicate the picture. I always felt a connection to that particular dragon and I imagined he was my protector whenever people would give me shit, he'd come in and flame them up." She sounded horrified, but I felt dizzy; as if I'd spent the past week on a binge.

I felt my face split in the widest grin the world would ever see. "*Really?* Do you want to give me a list of who I need to scorch now or do want to give it to me later? Because I'm down to do that in your honor."

"Oh god! Why is this happening? Your childhood crush finding out you tattooed his fucking picture on your ankle. Who else would that happen to but me?"

"You had a crush on me?" I asked, not even attempting to hide the excitement.

"Oh fuck! Why did I say that?" Her cheeks reddened. "Why am I still talking!"

"You had a crush on a dragon; you know how weird that it is, right? I mean, I'm flattered; but you are still super weird since you thought I was fictitious." Man, I wanted to kiss her.

Something scrapped against the metal of the front door; something with large claws was trying to dig in. I reached out and yanked Ana with actual force this time until she was pressed into my chest. My dragon nature roaring forward as anger filled me. Through sheer will, I managed to focus enough to think and not just react in dragon-sized wrath.

"Playtime is over. Time to get moving," I practically

growled; my arms tight around her body, the only thing keeping me from going berserk. Her admission that she had deliberately gotten my image, was doing nothing to damper the Draco bond that was swirling inside me.

She pulled from my embrace, only to put her hand in mine and head for the back. I reached over and snatched the ammo filled bag from the counter.

"Thanks," she called over her shoulder. "We can leave through here.

I stepped around her, handing her the backpack. "Hold this for a second."

She took it without hesitation. I quickly lifted the barriers I had created from the door, then took the pack back from her.

"Stay behind me unless the threat is there."

I saw her about to say something. I shook my head, cutting her off.

"Don't argue with me about it, it's non-negotiable."

She nodded. "Okay."

The scratching at the front door grew louder.

"Time to fly," I barked.

"Can you?" The hope in her voice was evident and it reminded me of the fact that she'd admitted to unknowingly on purpose getting me tattooed on her because she'd had a crush on me. The old magic flared in me.

"Nope. Not currently anyway. I'm working on it." I pulled open the door and peered out. "All clear back here so far.

I led Ana down the back alleyways, keeping close to the shadows. I had no idea where I could take her that she'd be safe from danger. I needed to regroup. My plan had fallen apart, starting with Jemma's death and deteriorated completely with the stone's missing location. My family and I never thought that the Goddess wouldn't have the Hearth Stone, let alone be dead and leave what appears to be an untrained goddess behind.

I suspected Ana had no idea what she was, and it was confirmed when she had been surprised of what I was and that I existed. I had no idea what I was going to do about the future of my family. All I knew was right now, I needed to get her as far as I could from the dimensional portal.

"We should go to the high school. Nobody will go there and I have a friend who works there that will help us." Her voice was in my ear while she pressed against my back in order to whisper.

Oh, Tatsu! She needed to back up. The serpent began to stir once more as if he'd forgotten he was trapped.

"Male friend?" I cringed and wanted to smack myself. Why did I say that? I'm an idiot.

I heard her giggle.

"Not that it matters. I mean I just need to know what I'm walking into," I added.

"Paola, has been a friend since forever. *She* is no danger to us." I could hear her still giggling.

I tried to deny to myself how relieved I felt. I couldn't explain why I felt how I felt about Ana, or what caused the bond; all I knew was that I had the urge to devour those who were around her, especially the male variety.

As we made our way to the high school, every once in a while, she'd place a hand against my back to slow me. It took me a few times to figure out what she was doing. She'd peek behind dumpsters to make sure nobody was there.

"Who are you looking for?" I finally asked her after

the fourth time.

"There is this guy I went to high school with who is sometimes out here. I wanted to make sure he wasn't stuck out here." She ducked behind the trash at the next building. "His favorite place is here, at the Green Fox Coffee shop, but he also likes the Sunshine Café or the Mountaintop Bar and Grill."

I nodded. "Okay. Which way to the high school?"

She stepped to my side. "Here, let's walk side by side and I can take you."

I was poised to fight, but she took my hand and her shoulder brushed against mine and I had nothing left to say. We quickly left the town square shopping area, Ana lead us away, not using the main streets and paths but taking me across shadowy fields and between buildings.

She stopped. "Is that a Burney Streamline? Like a legit one not a restoration?"

I let her hand drop from mine as I walked over it and trailed my fingertips. "Looks like it."

"Wow." She breathed. "Come on."

She started walking again and I didn't follow right away. Instead, I walked around the car out of place and time. Must be a time warp caused by the event. What else did the event cause and how many of us crossed over?

"Ka, come on," Ana whispered. I looked for her and saw her with her arm out stretched in my direction. Her fingers wiggled for me to take her hand.

"Give me just a second," I called back and went back to inspecting the temporal ripple.

"What's wrong?" Ana asked, once more at my side. I almost slipped my arm around her waist easily before I snapped out of it. I felt too comfortable with her. I was also all too aware of her palm pressed against my shoulder as she leaned in to look where I was looking.

"If my guess is correct this is a time distortion. We need to be careful. I've seemed to not taken in all that could happen with the celestial event." This time I did put my arm around her. "We better get moving."

We finally reached a building that Ana declared to be the school. I could feel the slight slump in her shoulders.

"What is it?"

She shook her head and stood up straight. "Nothing. I haven't stepped foot in this place since graduation. I better call Paola just to make sure she is here or tell her to come and meet us."

She pulled her phone from her pocket and peeked at it. "Shit! I missed her call." She stepped away from the so called safety of my arm and hit return missed call.

Even though she walked a little bit away, I could make out everything she said even as I scouted the area to make sure nothing from any other dimension was lurking around.

I needed to find a way to reach my sister Sui-Riu. I would probably have an easier time contacting Fuku, but he would try to come over and take over everything. I didn't want to admit that I had ulterior motives for nor wanting him over here—I didn't want him to lay eyes on Ana.

"Okay, she is here in her class room. She said we can come on up."

I jumped at the sound of her voice. Great. I'm sure that instilled confidence in my ability to protect her.

"What were you thinking about?" She teased. "You are turning bright red."

"Uh, nothing. Well, my siblings—my twin sister and my oldest brother specifically and which one would be more help."

"You have a twin sister?" Her excited smile was contagious. I let her loop her arm through the crook of my elbow and pull me up the steps and through the double doors.

"Yeah, I do. She is actually my best friend. Sui wanted to come over with me but Ri and Kin refused the idea," I sulked.

"Why did they do that? I mean they probably knew you could handle it, but a little help is always nice," she rambled as she navigated the halls of the school.

I snorted and a plume of smoke puffed out from my nostrils. "Oh! Sorry about that."

"What was that?" She laughed and leaned into me to bump against my side briefly.

"In this form I can't breathe fire, but that happens from time to time," I admitted light-heartedly, only because she seemed to be enjoying this so much. "And my family feels just the opposite of why Sui couldn't come. We are sort of the family screw ups. They thought we'd get distracted, find trouble and lose all hope of getting our wings back." I shrugged like it didn't bother me.

"I can't see you doing that. You seem so…I don't know." She scrunched her face up and looked like a playful bunny. "You seem super serious to me."

"Nah, they are right Sui and I always get into trouble. We are the youngest. The only two eggs in our clutch semi-attached and hatched at the exact same time. I remember seeing a hatchling next to me, but I couldn't get to her. We broke through the wall separating our eggs first and then we popped out the outer shell together. My family has learned that when there is trouble to be had, I go get Sui first. So, yeah, that is why there was no way in hell would they let me bring her for this. I can't afford any distraction." Too bad I found an even bigger one here, all without Sui's help. This one was actually dangerous because I wasn't sure what I was even capable of doing when it came to Ana. I wasn't even sure how much stronger the bond could get and I already felt this strongly about her after this short amount of time.

Ana stopped in front of a door, but that didn't stop her from rapping her knuckles on the door softly. The woman in the room with her short curly hair clipped back from her face looked up. She was pretty enough, I'm sure a lot of men found her drop dead gorgeous, but I was comparing her to Ana. The comparison was probably unfair because no woman on this Earth or any other held a flame to her.

"Ocean!" The woman threw her arms out and bum rushed us. She nudged me out the way and Ana released her hold on me to return the taller woman's hug.

"Paola, don't call me that! You sound like my mother except you are butchering it." Ana was trying to sound angry, but even I could tell it held no heat.

"Why is she calling you ocean?" I asked walking around the room, tapping the various things absently. I spun the globe, then moved on as it rotated.

Paola finally realized that someone else was here. She slid her large glasses up her nose as she inspected me.

"That's her name. Who is he?" She pointed at me, looking at Ana.

"This is Ka-Riu." She turned to me. "That's not my name. Well it kind of is my first name is Oshun. I go by my middle name. Anyway, this crazy nerd is Paola, my bestie since grammar school."

I nodded. "Nice to meet you."

She gave a small wave. "He's cute." I knew she was trying to whisper and she had no idea I could hear her as loud as if she were speaking in her regular octave.

"Shhhh!" Ana hissed.

"Have you seen anything crazy around here?" I asked, getting to the point I needed to know.

Paola went over to the nearest desk and sat down and Ana followed suit. There was no way I was going to be able to fit into one so I walked over to the larger desk, placing the backpack on it and leaned against it with my arms folded. I stayed hyper aware in case any form of danger showed up.

"I mean, I felt the earthquake. Maybe one of the mines collapsed." She gestured out the window. "I saw flashes and fire ball things over by your shop. I tried to call you, but you didn't answer and then the phone lines stopped working for a little. What the hell is going on?" Her voice was terse and held authority like she expected one of us to answer and do it quickly.

"You certainly sound like a high school teacher. I had my doubts, but I guess I can see it." Ana's grin was wide and lopsided.

"Shut up." Paola rolled her eyes, but I can tell she wasn't angry at all.

"Is Abrams alright? Is he still at the University? Are they okay over there?" Ana reached out and took her friend's hand. I sat and observed their exchange silently. I was trying to work out a plan—rather, it was a to-do list.

I needed to first, contact Sui-Riu, then I needed to

figure out where the hell the Hearth Stone was located and retrieve it.

"Yeah, he does that from time to time. Just zones out." I barely registered Ana's voice. Who was she talking about? I noticed that they were both staring at me. I snapped to attention. Ana looked amused and Paolo just stared at me, searching my face as if she were dissecting every little flaw I had.

"Sorry, did you say something to me?" I tried to pretend that I wasn't embarrassed.

"Yes," she laughed. "Thinking about your family again?"

I nodded. "How did you know?"

She stood up and I tried not to zero in on the way her hips did this little dance as she made her way over to me.

"You get this adorable look on your face when you do. Part pained, part worry and part annoyance." She stopped incredibly close to me. I think it was so she could speak to me without her friend overhearing.

"That pretty much explains how I feel exactly when I think about my family," I admitted. Without thinking, I reached forward and placed my hand on her hip. She didn't seem to notice, or if she did, it didn't bother her so she didn't react to it. Wait. Actually, she *did*. She leaned into me slightly.

I really should take my hand back, but that was so not going to happen. I couldn't make myself even if I wanted to do it.

"Any ideas on what to do next? How do we contact Sui?" She looked up into my face, expecting me to have some sort of answer. I hated to disappoint her, so my brain scrambled to think of something.

AH!

"There is a chemistry lab in this school right?" I asked excitedly and Ana mirrored my smile.

"Yes, do you need to borrow it?"

"Yup. I'll also need some supplies. We'll need alkaline water, coal, obsidian and any rock as long as it has an iron concentrate." I rattled off and Ana pulled from my touch and went over to Paola, who typed on her phone. I didn't hear what she told her because I was too busy trying to work out how I was going to cause a rift to open.

"Okay I know where to get that stuff come on." She took my hand and took off out the room, dragging me behind her. I had mere moments to scoop up her bag.

Acknowledgements

I want to give a big shout out to all the people who helped me finish this book.

To all the amazing authors involved in the Saint's Grove project; it's been a pleasure working with you. A big nod to Carly Fall for inviting me in the first place.

My beta readers, Vicki Jacobs and Stephen Garinger. Your time is invaluable.

Julie Titus, formatter extraordinaire. You help me rock it.

Doreen Shababy, my Mommy and biggest fan. Even if you're the only one who ever reads my books, I think I'll keep writing them.

Dorothy Dunn. I miss you every day, Grams.

My boys, Quinton and Leeland, for always thinking I'm smarter than I am.

Scott Miller… thank you for adding a little magic to my world.

Mary Malone, friend and editor. I couldn't do any of this without you.

Jennifer Malone Wright... as always, you are my inspiration, best friend, sister, and hetero lifemate. Someday when we're old and gray, I know we'll be causing trouble and creating mayhem. I can't wait.

ABOUT THE AUTHOR

R ose Shababy lives in eastern Washington State. She grew up in the Northwest but swears she's going to move to warmer climates someday. She's claimed this for over 20 years, however, and has yet to move more than 75 miles away from her mother.

Rose has a deep love of all things Star Trek and yearns to travel the heavens, as well as an intense desire to be bitten by a radioactive spider. Unfortunately she sucks at science and math so she hasn't been able bring her dreams to life, instead living vicariously through books, comics, television and film. She hopes to someday make a million dollars so she can afford to buy her way to the international space station, but she'd settle for being able to fly around the world and leap tall buildings in a single bound.

Rose also loves to cook and worked for years in a gourmet Italian grocery and deli where she learned to hone her skills. She often prepares culinary masterpieces, but fervently wishes the dishes would wash themselves. Especially now that her dishwashers/children are grown and no longer live at home.

Rose likes to use her free time wisely. For instance, she likes to daydream, will often read for hours until she falls asleep on the couch with an electric blanket and a warm tabby cat curled up on her hip, as well as spending cozy weekend days watching Syfy movies like Sharknado and Mega Piranha.

If Rose were a cartoon animal, she'd prefer to be a wise old owl or a sleek and sexy jaguar, but in reality she'd probably be a myopic mole with coke-bottle glasses.